Not My Affair

Not My Affair

Pamela Fudge

ROBERT HALE · LONDON

Typeset in Sabon
Printed and bound in Great Britain by TJ International Ltd

Dedication

This book is dedicated to the memory of the real Gemma, Sadie and Zoe who I often met on the daily walks I took with my own dog, little Gizmo (Gizmo featured in an earlier book, *Not What It Seems*) and they – and their owner, Carol – never failed to brighten our day.

Acknowledgements

My thanks go to all at Robert Hale Ltd, who gave me my start as an author and have continued to believe in me. Thank you to my daughter, Kelly, for providing me with the title of this book and, in doing so, saving me a lot of thinking time.

I am blessed every day to have the love and support of my lovely family, my children, Shane, Kelly, Scott, not forgetting Mike and Jess and my gorgeous grandchildren, Abbie, Emma, Tyler, Bailey, Mia and our newest addition, Lewis.

Also thanks to my sisters, Barb and Pat, my stepdaughter, Rachel, and my web-master and stepson, Mark, who count among my regular readers as do my wonderful friends Pam M, Pam W, Karen, Chris N, Chris H, Nora, Sheila, Jan, Angela, Helen, Sally and Dex, and to Margaret and Maurice, Beverley and Anna who have been so supportive.

Chapter One

I HELD THE BEAUTIFULLY wrapped gift in my hands, loving the very obvious effort Jack had put into making the packaging special. Turning it over, touching the trailing ribbons, I read again the label written in Jack's strong scrawl and melted as I savoured the loving words.

For My Beautiful Wife, Wishing You a Merry Christmas, Fay, it said, *Forever Yours, Jack.*

With almost twenty years of marriage behind us, I couldn't fail to be touched and only hoped the next twenty would be as good. I had a strong feeling they were going to be even better.

Smiling up at him I said, 'For an accountant you have a wonderful way with words, darling husband.'

'Open it, Fay. Go on, open it,' he urged, ever impatient. 'It's your birthstone, I chose it especially.'

Jack leaned over the back of my chair to savour the moment as the paper fell away and I slowly lifted the lid of a long slim box lined with cream silk. We both stared down at the single item nestling inside for the longest moment. Then I felt my whole world tilt on its axis, leaving me feeling sick to my stomach and so shaken that I felt physically ill. The silence swirling around us was so thick it could have been cut with a knife.

The piece of jewellery was a pendant. It was absolutely beautiful and had obviously cost a great deal of money. However, I didn't have to point out that the stone wasn't the opal for the month of my birth that we had obviously both been expecting to see, given Jack's confident words. In fact, I was pretty sure emerald was the birthstone for someone born in May, months away from my October birthday.

When I looked up at Jack, his stricken expression confirmed what I was trying so hard not to accept – despite the unmistakable and damning evidence to the contrary. I was definitely *not* the intended recipient for this particular and very expensive present.

'I can explain,' he said, desperation in his voice, and guilt written all over his good-looking face.

'I'd like to see you try,' I replied, without a trace of humour, 'and don't even think of blaming the jeweller for giving you the wrong necklace, because we both know that's not what happened. How very unimaginative of you to buy similar presents for your wife and your mistress, Jack, and then become careless enough to mix them up during the wrapping process, because that's what's happened here, isn't it?

'You may be wondering why I'm not asking who she is, but that's not really what's important, is it? The fact that she even exists is what matters. Just go, Jack.' I was amazed at how steady my voice was. 'Go on, pack your bags, get out of this house and out of my life – and take this with you.' I thrust the box, together with its contents and packaging back into his unwilling hands. 'I can't even bear to look at you.'

'You can't mean that,' he pleaded. 'Where do you expect me to go? It's Christmas day, Fay.'

'Oh, yes, so it is. What do you want me to say – Merry Christmas, Jack? There, I've said it and now you can go.'

I didn't move from the chair. I wouldn't have known how to. I sensed rather than saw him move to the door, and then pause there. I couldn't even be bothered to look at him.

'Are you sure this is what you want – really certain that you want me to leave? Can't we even talk about this?'

I ignored him, and eventually I heard his muffled footsteps on the carpeted stairs and then the sound of cupboards and drawers opening and closing. Finally, the click of the front door told me that he had gone and, as quickly and simply as that, my marriage was over.

I sat without moving for a very long time. I understood that I was in shock, because it was almost exactly how I had felt when my father died suddenly, leaving me stunned and incapable of rational thought. I hadn't been expecting his life to end so abruptly, not when he had seemed to be so hale and hearty – just like my marriage to Jack.

Unsuspected heart disease had brought about my father's demise and an unsuspected affair had spelled the abrupt end of my marriage. In both cases I was left with the question, why didn't I know?

Obviously I hadn't been aware that my father was ill because there were no apparent signs, apart from the fact he had less energy, which was hardly surprising for a man in his seventies.

The same couldn't be said about Jack and his affair, I was beginning to realize, because the longer I thought about it – and I found it impossible to think about anything else – the signs had all been there right in front of me. The only surprise was that I *hadn't* noticed because they were the very ones that all the newspaper columns, magazines articles and TV and radio programmes warned you about.

I found that I was taunting myself about that sudden urgent desire for a gym membership, when Jack had never been anything less than fit anyway, and the avid interest in clothes from a man who had always detested shopping and been more than happy to leave replenishing his wardrobe to me. If that hadn't been enough there was the new cologne – chosen without my help – and the leap to getting his fair hair cut into a Gary Barlow style after favouring the same, far more practical style, for more years than I cared to remember. Put all those things together and it should have been a dead giveaway.

Now I could understand the changes of mood, which we had both blamed on pressure at work, and the late meetings and weekend conferences which suddenly became more frequent, and the fact I could never reach Jack on a mobile, which was constantly switched off or without a signal.

'You,' I told myself abruptly, 'have been an absolute bloody idiot.'

Galvanized into action by the anger that suddenly roared through me, I thrust myself out of the chair. The Christmas tree mocking me with its twinkling lights was the first thing to go. Somehow I resisted the urge to tear into it, destroying what we had decorated together – recalling very much against my will how we had laughed with genuine relief when the lights actually worked and then opened the chilled champagne when the crystal star was set in place, right at the very top, signalling the completion of a job well done.

Instead I systematically stripped the tree, dropping treasured decorations we had purchased together over the years of our marriage into a black bag without a second thought. The tinsel and lights followed, and then the tree itself – a healthy green and with all the needles still intact – was dragged outside and placed next to the bin.

'I know they're messy things, but isn't Christmas day a bit soon to be taking your tree down?'

I cursed under my breath as I turned to face old Mrs Bramshaw. She was just tall enough to peer over the fence, especially when she stood on tip-toe as she was obviously doing at that moment.

'Hay fever,' I offered abruptly by way of explanation, careless of the fact it was virtually impossible to suffer from that particular affliction in the United Kingdom in December.

'Oh dear,' she began, and then after a moment's thought, 'but ...'

I was back indoors before she had finished speaking, closing the door firmly behind me. I suppose I could have simply told her that the festivities were over in the Ryan household – due to the fact that it had recently been revealed the husband had been investigating stockings other than the ones hanging over his own hearth – but I was sure she would find out soon enough.

Methodically all traces of Christmas were erased from the house, the holly wreath on the front door, the ivy twisted around the banister rails, and the mistletoe attached to the light fittings. I did actually give a thought to the starving in the world as I cleared out the fridge but, deciding that this was one occasion when it was important to put my own needs first, the festive food all went the way of everything else.

Stripping the king-sized bed, I was ruthless in dismissing images from my mind of how we had celebrated waking up to what was going to be another perfect Christmas day together.

By the time I had bagged up the clothes Jack hadn't taken

with him, I was running out of black sacks and running out of the incandescent rage that had driven me up to this point. I resisted the urge to take a pair of sharp scissors to any of his belongings, or even to load them into the car and drop them at the nearest charity shop, knowing those things had all been done many times before. The one thing I had left to me was my dignity – and that I was grimly determined to hold onto at all costs.

I piled the bags into the downstairs cloakroom, closing the door with difficulty before returning to my chair in the sitting room. I sat down to decide what my next move would be, and that was when the doorbell rang and went on ringing. I sat motionless. I had no intention of answering the door, perfectly sure it would be a remorseful Jack, probably recovering from the shock of being caught out and determined to wheedle his way back in.

The letterbox rattled. 'Fay? Jack? What's going on? Open the door.'

I couldn't think for the life of me what my mother was doing here, but I did know that she wouldn't give up and go away.

Using the arms of the chair to lever myself to my feet again, I made my way to the door. I felt as if I had aged ten years now that anger was no longer fuelling my actions and was amazed when I passed the hall mirror to discover that I looked exactly the same. My dark hair was still smooth and silky, make-up still in place and my festive little black dress, though a little creased, still looked – well – festive.

I opened the door and my mother bustled in, talking all the while.

'I waited,' she complained, 'and then I phoned and got no answer, and in the end I just got a taxi. Have you any idea how difficult it is to get a taxi on Christmas Day, Fay?' She came to an abrupt halt in the sitting room doorway and was stunned into silence for what was, for her, a very long time. Then she turned to me and asked in a puzzled tone, 'What happened to Christmas?'

'I discovered Jack's having an affair,' I said, as if that explained everything – and to me it did.

For a second time my mother didn't know what to say. She wasn't often lost for words and never for very long.

'Who with?'

I shrugged.

'Where is he?'

'Gone.'

She looked scandalized at that. 'He's *left* you?'

'No, I told him to go.'

'Why?'

I stared at her. 'Didn't you hear me? I said he's having an affair.'

'Marriages do survive affairs, dear,' she pointed out in what she obviously imagined was a reasonable tone.

'Not this one,' I said firmly. 'Now, can we talk about something else, please?'

'Can I just say that you seem to be taking this remarkably calmly, before we change the subject?' She looked at me closely and then bustled past me into the kitchen. 'I'll put the kettle on, shall I?'

Without waiting for an answer, she did just that, while I trailed behind her and watched from the doorway. Setting out the tray with cups and saucers, she didn't come unstuck until she opened the fridge door and then she straightened up and stared at me.

'There's no milk,' she said, carefully ignoring the fact

that the whole fridge had been emptied of anything that was remotely edible.

I cleared my throat. 'Erm, I might have thrown that out along with everything else.'

'*Why?*'

'Because it seemed to me entirely appropriate, under the circumstances, to simply cancel Christmas,' I said, turning away and returning to my chair in the sitting room.

'I think you're in shock,' my mother said, following me. 'You had no idea, had you?'

I shook my head. 'None at all.'

She went to the drinks cabinet and, probably surprised and relieved to find the contents of that were still intact, she poured two generous helpings of brandy and handed one to me.

'Cheers and a very merry Christmas,' I said bitterly, holding the glass aloft and then downing the contents in one. It took just a second before the fiery liquid hit the back of my throat and then I couldn't breathe. My eyes streamed as I coughed and spluttered and fought to catch my breath. Without a word, my mother handed me a tissue from the box on the coffee table and then went into the hall to answer the phone I hadn't even noticed was ringing.

'Oh, it's you,' she snapped and then her side of the conversation became muffled as she tried to have her say without me overhearing.

I watched her through the crack in the door, walking backwards and forwards, her back rigid with anger. Poor Mum, I thought, arriving under her own steam for what she was expecting to be a pleasant Christmas day with her only daughter and son-in-law and finding herself suddenly caught up in the crossfire of a marriage in crisis.

She was dressed for the festive occasion in smart black

trousers, no doubt with a cream silk blouse underneath the scarlet wool coat that she had yet to remove. Her blonde hair was an artfully arranged tumble of curls, a style far too young for a woman approaching her seventies, and I knew without checking that her make-up would be immaculate. This was the face my mother had been resolutely showing to the world since my father had died five years before and – the thought suddenly came to me that if she could do it, then so could I. The circumstances weren't too dissimilar, after all.

'Well, you've shocked me, Jack,' she suddenly admitted sharply, forgetting to keep her voice down, 'and I thought I was past the age of being shocked about anything. What possessed you?'

It was a shame I couldn't hear his reply.

'How do you think she is? It's not often the demise of a marriage comes in a gift-wrapped parcel on Christmas Day. Actually, Jack,' Mum hissed furiously after a brief pause while she listened, 'why don't you tell her that yourself?'

Before I had time to gather my wits she was standing in front of me, holding the phone out.

'No, no.' I shrank back into the chair, holding my hands out in front of me, palms forward as if to ward off the instrument. 'I don't want to talk to him.'

'Speak to him,' she ordered in a tone that brooked no argument, 'he *is* still your husband, Fay, whatever he's been up to and however you feel about it.' With that she dropped the receiver into my lap, picked up her handbag and said over her shoulder as she left, 'I'm going to see if I can find a shop open.'

The front door clicked quietly behind her and I stared down at the phone. It was seeing my hand tremble as I reached to pick it up that sent some much needed anger flooding through my veins and the reminder that *I* had actually done nothing wrong.

'What do you want?' I was pleased with the flat tone, devoid of any expression.

'I was worried about you,' Jack said and, in spite of myself, I found I was on the verge of melting at the sound of his voice and the fact that he obviously still cared, until I reminded myself that worrying about me hadn't stopped him embarking on an affair behind my back.

'You don't have to worry about me, I'll be fine.'

'I didn't mean for any of this to happen, Fay.'

'No?' I posed it as a question. 'But you must know that "this" is what happens, Jack, when one partner cheats on the other. We've seen approximately half of our friends' and colleagues' relationships fall apart because one of them played away from home.'

'It was really horrible,' he admitted, 'the way you found out. I wouldn't have had that happen for the world.'

'I'm sure you wouldn't, but if you hadn't been having an affair in the first place, Jack,' my voice was intentionally brusque, 'there would have been nothing for me to find out.'

'You sound so cold,' Jack said, 'so unfeeling.'

I was glad I was able to give that impression. I had been a party to enough break-ups over the years to be familiar with the pattern that followed – the endless recriminations, the demand for details, revenge tactics that ranged from the trashing of prized possessions to actual bodily harm. Nothing good had ever come from it and the majority of relationships never recovered anyway.

I had watched my mother come to terms with losing my father and this, as I'd already realized, wasn't so very different – apart, of course, from the fact that my father had no choice in the matter and Jack did.

I hardened my heart, built another protective shell around it and asked, 'Why have you phoned, Jack? You obviously made your choices some time ago and this is the result. I can't really see what else there is to talk about – apart from who gets what in the divorce.'

I heard his swift intake of breath and felt my own breathing falter at something I hadn't actually considered at all, not until that very moment. It was unbelievable to recall that we had woken up that morning to all intents and purposes an extremely happily married couple, and that before nightfall our marriage was damaged beyond repair.

'You can't mean it. I didn't think it would come to this.'

'Probably because you didn't think at all, did you?'

'It was a silly fling, Fay. Honestly, it meant nothing. I promise you, it's over and nothing like it will ever happen again.'

But it had meant enough for him to buy whoever she was a very expensive bauble for Christmas, identical to the one he had bought for his own wife – except for the one very important detail that had been his downfall. And maybe the affair was over, but I didn't need to ask how recently it had ended or that Jack clumsily giving the game away was the *only* reason it had ended.

'Just let me know when you would like to collect your things, Jack,' I said, suddenly tiring of what was a completely pointless conversation, 'and I will make sure I'm out.'

He was babbling when I pressed the red button on the phone and in the silence that followed I sat very still, staring straight ahead, wondering again how on earth it had come to this.

I didn't hear my mother come in the front door – she must

have taken the spare key from the hook – and I jumped when it slammed behind her. The sudden movement sent the telephone receiver slipping from my lap and down the side of the chair. I delved down to retrieve it and when I pulled the phone out, a small parcel gaily wrapped followed, the ribbon caught around my fingers.

I didn't have to guess at the content because I had wrapped the gift myself and would have given it to Jack the minute I'd finished opening his present to me – if everything hadn't all gone so horribly wrong.

The tears came as my mother came round the sitting room door, triumphantly brandishing a bulging carrier bag with the name of a convenience store emblazoned on the side. The bag was dropped as she watched my composure disintegrate in front of her eyes.

'What's he done now?' she demanded, her voice shrill. 'What's he said?'

I shook my head helplessly, finally experiencing the full force of a pain that the initial shock had been shielding me from, and howled my grief as I handed my mother the tiny parcel.

Turning it over in her hands until the label could be seen, she stared at it and then at me. '"To Jack,' she read out loud, 'I didn't have to guess what you'd like for Christmas because I know this is what you've always wanted,' and then slowly my mother untied the ribbon and parted the paper.

'Oh, Fay,' she said, tears already streaming down her own face. 'Oh, Fay.'

In her hands lay a pair of snow white bootees.

Chapter Two

M Y MOTHER HELD the tiny bootees close to her face, but carefully so as to avoid allowing the fat tears that rolled down her cheeks, or the make-up so carefully applied that morning to spoil the soft white wool. She – of all people – knew what that little gift meant. It meant that for Jack and me the years of waiting were finally over and a longed for baby was on its way for us – except, of course, that now there was no 'us'.

'Jack doesn't know?' she whispered.

I shook my head. 'Wrapping those up for him was my way of breaking the news.'

As I spoke I was assuring myself that the grief I felt wasn't for me. No, the grief I felt was all for this innocent little baby, being born into a home that wasn't just broken, but smashed to smithereens almost from the time that he or she was conceived. In fact – and the realization hit me like a brutal slap in the face – the affair had almost certainly been going on when our own love-making had created this child.

The sudden sour taste that flooded my mouth at the thought made me gag. I staggered to my feet and rushed to the downstairs loo where I was forced to clamber over Jack's bagged up belongings to reach the toilet before I could even throw up. The brandy made me cough just as much when it made its reappearance as it had when I drank it so eagerly, and I realized belatedly that my pregnant state meant the comfort of alcohol was something I was going to have to forgo for the foreseeable future.

My mother had made me sweet milky tea in my absence and I took the cup and wrapped my cold hands around it, gratefully looking for comfort of any kind anywhere I could find it.

'What will you do?' she asked.

'Do?' I stared at her, and for the first time my stunned gaze took in the ruined make-up, messy hair, crumpled clothes and anxious eyes that had turned my mother into a stranger just when I most needed her to be the strong woman she had always been.

It was as if she'd actually read my thoughts and I watched her make a supreme effort to pull herself together. She checked her reflection in the mirror and made a feeble attempt to repair some of the damage before turning to face me again.

'You're going to have to talk to Jack, Fay,' she said firmly, 'and you're going to have to tell him – about the baby. Whatever has happened it is his child, too, you know.'

'He doesn't deserve a child,' I said, and surprised even myself with the unmistakable venom in my tone.

'Perhaps not,' she kept her voice carefully neutral, 'but at this present moment he is still your husband and, whatever he has done, he will always be the baby's father.'

I nodded, accepting both facts with difficulty. 'Yes, all right, I know I will have to tell him, sooner or later, and I understand the pregnancy will rather complicate things. It won't simply be a case of dividing everything up and going our separate ways.'

'Darling, don't you think – for the sake of the child – you should make at least some attempt to work things out with Jack?'

I shook my head. 'No.' The word was simple and emphatic.

I thought she was going to argue but, obviously seeing that my mind was made up, my mother walked away muttering something about putting together a meal for us, leaving me to ponder the realities of what my life might be as a single mother.

The house would have to be sold, of course, but that wasn't the end of the world after all – though once, only a ridiculously short time ago, I would have thought it was. From the day we moved in, I'd truly believed it was our forever home but, since it obviously hadn't meant the same to Jack, the thought of leaving it wasn't the wrench I might have expected it to be.

The property was obviously worth quite a lot and the mortgage, thankfully, had long since been paid off. It was a very beautiful house, and we had spent a lot of time and money over the years making it into the perfect family home. That was in the days when we hadn't a doubt that having a family was nothing more than a matter of time.

I tried not to think about those days and reminded myself instead that, with house prices as they were, the sale of this one should provide quite enough for the purchase of two rather smaller homes. A bachelor flat for Jack, who had opted for the single life, and a two bedroom cottage or apartment for me and our baby – not quite what I'd envisaged for life in my forties, but I would make sure the child didn't miss out on anything.

I stood up suddenly, telling myself I'd done enough thinking. I didn't intend to play the victim here. What had happened to me happened to women – and men, too – every day of the week and I had to learn to accept the unacceptable and move on with my life.

I went upstairs and cleansed my face of what was left of my make-up. My eyes were red and puffy, but I told myself the time for tears was already over – I had a child to think of. Jack was old enough to think for himself – he'd already demonstrated that very clearly.

My mother looked up when I walked into the kitchen, her gaze taking in the neatly brushed shoulder-length hair, the change into comfortable clothes and the face devoid of make-up. I hope she'd also noticed the determined expression, because I was sure it was quite similar to the one I often saw on her face when she was about to tackle a daunting task.

Her smile was crooked. 'You look as if you're about to attempt Everest,' she said, 'but please remember that you don't have to do it alone. You have me. You'll always have me.'

She pulled a chair out for me at the kitchen table and I sat down. As she placed beans on toast in front of me, I couldn't help reflecting that this had to be the oddest Christmas Day I had ever spent and hopefully the only one of its kind I was ever likely to experience.

As she joined me and we began to eat, my mother offered an apology for the meagre fare. 'I'm sorry, I know this isn't much but, according to the magazines I've read in recent times, there seems to be so many things these days that a pregnant woman isn't supposed to eat. I was quite at a loss without having a list of some sort to hand.'

I managed to dredge up a smile from somewhere, because I didn't have to remind myself that none of this was her fault.

'It's fine, Mum,' I assured her, 'I'd forgotten how tasty beans on toast can be.'

We ate without speaking for a while, just the scrape of cutlery on china was breaking the silence.

'Are you sure...?' my mother began at one point.

'I'm sure,' I anticipated the rest of her question, 'that I don't want him·back – not now or at any time in the future. You must see that it would never work, because quite simply I could never, ever trust him again. I really don't want to spend the rest of my life wondering what Jack is up to behind my back. I've seen it all before, Mum – watched friends' relationships crumble under the barrage of questions about where he or she has been and why a simple errand took him or her ten minutes longer than it should, then there's the phone checking, going through pockets looking for suspicious receipts – and these affairs are rarely a one-off. Once there's a taste for it ...' I left the rest unsaid.

'To be fair,' she pointed out, 'Jack didn't know you were pregnant. I'm sure he wouldn't have dreamed ...'

'... of cheating on a pregnant wife? Perhaps not, but it shouldn't have made any difference whether I was pregnant or not, should it? Now,' I put my knife and fork down neatly, side by side, 'you are not to tell him – or anyone else, Mum – about the baby. I will do it, but not until I'm good and ready.'

'But—' she began.

'There are no buts,' I said firmly. 'I didn't ask for any of this to happen, but now I must deal with it as I see fit. It's important for the baby that I don't get stressed, and it's important to me that I behave with dignity. I've seen too many friends make complete idiots of themselves in similar circumstances and, I can tell you straight, that isn't going to happen to me.'

'If it's just your pride making you refuse to see Jack ...' my mother began again.

'My pride and my baby,' I told her, 'and, at this moment, I

feel they're all I have left. Please allow me to do this my way.'

She looked at me for a long moment, and then nodded slowly. 'And me,' she said, a reminder of what she had said earlier, 'you have me. You'll always have me, Fay.'

Despite it still being relatively early, we took ourselves off to bed soon after that. I couldn't speak for my mother but I felt absolutely and utterly exhausted. Providing her with an armful of fresh bedding for the spare room, I left her to it. There was no question of her returning home that night and neither of us even suggested it. Finding a taxi or getting out the car would have taken far too much effort and, anyway, from my point of view, it was nice to know there was someone else in the house.

The longer I lay awake, staring into the darkness, the more the day's events took on a dreamlike quality. As when my father had died, I became more and more convinced that, if I slept at all, when I woke in the morning I would find Jack asleep in bed beside me and realize the whole episode had been no more than a particularly nasty nightmare.

In fact, I woke to winter sun streaming into the bedroom and, looking at the clock, was amazed to find I'd slept late into the morning. I was immediately aware – without turning over – that Jack's side of the bed had not been slept in and had no trouble at all remembering why. The shocking events of the day before came hurtling back with painful clarity and a hefty helping of complete disbelief, but I wasted only a brief moment of wishing things could have been different before realizing how pointless that was.

What I needed, I told myself firmly, was to be up and doing something constructive with the day ahead. There were plans to be made and no time to waste as far as I was concerned. Throwing back the duvet, I shook my head to empty it of all the might-have-been thoughts and instead made my mind up to prepare a to-do list.

I didn't give any consideration at all to what my mother might be doing as I went from en-suite shower to walk-in wardrobe, just assumed she was either sleeping in as well or keeping busy downstairs. Taking a leaf from her well-established book of tips on how to survive a crisis, I worked hard at making myself presentable. Just because I was going to be an older mother-to-be at thirty-nine, and a single mother to boot, I reminded myself, there was no reason to let myself go.

I had trouble with the list – so perhaps I wasn't quite as clear-headed as I would like to have believed. In the end it was very short, to the point and consisted only of:

Make appointment with solicitor
Arrange for estate agent to call

Those two items alone were enough to fill me with disbelief, that the marriage I had always thought so solid really was over on the one hand, and a determination not to delay the inevitable repercussions on the other. What was done was done and couldn't be undone as far as I was concerned, it was best just to get on and deal with the consequences of my husband's actions and not waste time wishing it had never happened.

That it was still only Boxing Day really surprised me because the dreadful events of Christmas Day seemed to have taken place such a long time ago. Even to myself, I seemed remarkably calm under the circumstances, but then watching my mother deal with a catastrophe that did have its similarities, in the past, was probably – no, actually definitely – helping. She had shown me that we could survive every one of the things life threw at us and were far stronger than we might ever have guessed.

I accepted that nothing could be done about the two items on the list right away because of the festive holiday closures that would affect both of those businesses, so I focussed on the matter in hand – which boiled down to making myself presentable for the day ahead.

I tried not to admit part of the reason this was so important to me was in case Jack turned up on the doorstep. The thought of seeing him made me quake a bit, but there was no way I was going to allow him to gain the impression that his actions had resulted in me falling apart.

I must have spent an hour primping, and it was more as a way of passing time than anything else, but I was pleased with the result. My arms ached from the effort I'd made with the straighteners but my dark hair hung long and glossy to my shoulders and, after I had applied my make-up with infinite care, I was even able to raise a small smile at my reflection.

Even to my critical eyes I thought I looked good and gave myself a firm nod of approval. Turning this way and that in front of the mirror I was able to convince myself there was no sign at all of a baby bump, not even in the skinny black jeans and bright cerise pink-ribbed sweater that I was wearing. Only as I walked out of my bedroom and onto the landing did I stop to consider that the complete silence in the rest of the house might be in any way ominous.

'Mum?' I called and receiving no answer, I called again but more sharply this time. 'Mum, where are you?'

The door of the spare room she'd used was slightly ajar, which I took as an indication that she was already up, so I went to the top of the stairs and listened. Only a very definite hush greeted me and I felt the beginning of the first real sense of unease.

I ran lightly down the stairs and straight into the kitchen, which a quick glance told me was still as spick and span as we'd left it when we retired to bed the night before.

Perhaps she'd gone to the shops again – the thought came and was quickly dismissed. Her coat was still hanging in the hall and, anyway, my mother did nothing in the morning without the cup of tea she swore set her up for the day, and the kettle was stone cold.

The sitting room and dining room were in the same pristine state. I was getting increasingly concerned as I went on to try the utility room and then the downstairs cloakroom with its mountain of black bags. From the conservatory I could see into the garden, the lawn with its covering of frost unmarked by the footprints that might have indicated my mother taking a morning stroll. Where the hell was she?

'Mother, Mother, where are you?' The words emerged shrill and panic-stricken from my lips and that was most definitely the way I was beginning to feel. A grown woman couldn't completely disappear, could she? Had she been kidnapped while I slept?

'Calm down and don't be so bloody ridiculous, Fay Ryan,' I said the words out loud, and took a few deep breaths in an attempt to slow the frantic beating of my heart.

Standing in the wide hallway, I reminded myself that I hadn't checked properly upstairs and found myself looking nervously up towards the landing. Gripping the banister rail tightly I made my way slowly up, step by step, all the while wondering what I was going to find. A fall in the shower, a slip in the bedroom, a diabetic coma – though to my knowledge my mother wasn't diabetic. In the end I tried not to think at all.

The bathroom clearly hadn't been used recently, no water splashes in the sink or on the shower stall, no damp towels in the laundry basket. I automatically straightened towels that already hung straight, closed the mirrored cabinet door that was slightly ajar and then, after one more glance round, I turned and made my way to the spare bedroom.

I thrust the door wide open so that it thumped against the wall behind it, and stepped inside. My hand flew immediately to my mouth and I gasped out loud. I could see my mother's huddled shape in the bed, but all that actually showed of her were a few tumbled curls peeping out above the duvet. I could detect no movement at all, no rise and fall of her breathing. Oh, God, she couldn't be dead, could she? She just couldn't be.

'Mum,' I whimpered, 'oh, Mum.'

I took a tentative step forward, my feet sinking into the thick carpet and a sob escaped from my lips. As I neared the bed, I reached out a hand and whispered again, 'Mum. Wake up. *Please* wake up.'

I was standing beside the bed, staring in disbelief at the still form of my mother, and my shaking hand had actually reached out and grasped the edge of the duvet, when the door-bell rang suddenly and I screamed long and loud.

Chapter Three

'WELL, I KNOW I'm probably not very welcome here,' Jack said from his position on the doorstep, looking rueful, 'but you look as if you've seen a ghost, Fay. It has only been twenty-four hours and I am still your husband. I came because I thought we should talk.'

I didn't speak for a moment and I couldn't have done if I'd tried. Not after my headlong flight down the stairs had left me breathless and light-headed. I was beginning to realize that, for the second time in as many days, I was also in deep shock.

'Has something happened?' Jack asked, looking at me more closely, blue eyes clouding with concern, and then he added as an afterthought, 'I mean, has something *else* happened?'

Finding Jack on the doorstep, after the traumatic discovery of his treachery only the day before, was my worst nightmare but also the answer to my prayers. Whatever I was going to have to face up there in my spare bedroom, at least I no longer had to do it alone. Jack was obviously taken aback to find himself being pulled into the hallway, and he stood there watching me curiously as I closed the door and turned to face him.

'It's my mother,' I told him, 'she's dead,' and then with

greater emphasis I repeated, 'she's *dead*,' and as the reality of the statement hit me like a speeding train, I burst into floods of tears.

'What the hell do you mean, dead? *Dead*?' He pulled a face and took a step back away from me to stare at me in very evident disbelief. 'Don't be silly. She can't possibly be dead. She was fine yesterday. Has there been an accident? Where is she?'

'Upstairs,' I sobbed, pointing up. 'She must have died in her sleep. I've only just found her.'

'Why was she in bed? Has she been ill?'

I shook my head. 'No, but with everything that's happened, we were both completely exhausted last night. I slept deeply and didn't wake until late this morning. I thought Mum was probably already up and about, so I took my time having a shower and getting dressed, but when I came downstairs there was no sign of her. I've only just looked into the spare room and found her lying there.' I couldn't stop crying and didn't bother to try.

'Let's go and check, shall we?' Jack was making an effort to sound unruffled but I could tell he was shaken. His face was bleached of its normal healthy colour and he kept raking agitated fingers through his fair hair, leaving it standing up in crazy spikes.

When he reached out a hand to me I placed my own into it immediately. All differences between us had to be put aside while we faced whatever waited for us in the silent room upstairs. I grasped the banister tightly with my other hand, and could feel the terrified thud of my heart like hammer blows against my ribs as every reluctant step took me closer.

Jack was the one who pulled back the duvet and we both looked down on my mother's dear face, even smoother and totally unlined now that the stresses of life had been erased.

'Oh, Mum,' I cried. Jack held his arms out and I melted into them, glad of his warmth and glad of his strength.

'You've still got me,' he said, but I shook my head against his jacket because even in my grief I couldn't begin to forgive him.

'No, Jack, I haven't – not anymore. Now there's only me.'

Pulling away, I stood gazing at my mother and wondered who else I was going to lose from my life. The thought made me close my arms protectively around my non-existent belly.

'Hey, just a minute ...'

When Jack spoke I thought for a moment that he had noticed and realized the significance of my action, but he was looking past me and peering hard at my mother.

'Iris,' he suddenly said very loudly. 'Iris, can you hear me?' He leaned over until his face was almost touching hers and then, before I could stop him, he had grasped the glass of water sitting on the bedside cabinet and dashed the contents into my mother's face.

'For God's sake, Jack,' I gasped, 'what the bloody hell do you think you're doing?'

I pushed him away, and had snatched up tissues and started to wipe away the trickling water, when my mother's eyes flew open so suddenly that I almost fell over backwards. I screamed and screamed, clutching at my chest with the shock of this unexpected sign of life.

'What?' she said, blinking against the light. Her voice came out blurry and thick from a sleep so deep that it had offered all the appearance of death.

'What – bloody *what*?' I yelled, relief making me so angry I think I could have killed her if I hadn't been so pleased that she was alive. 'You frightened the life out of me – out of us. We thought you were dead.'

'Dead?' she struggled to sit up. 'Don't be so ridiculous. There's nothing in the world wrong with me.'

'But it's almost lunchtime and I couldn't wake you.'

'Oh.' Realization appeared to dawn. My mother struggled to sit up and then reached for a bottle of pills sitting on the bedside cupboard and held them out to me. 'I couldn't get off to sleep last night, so I took one of these. I found them in the bathroom cabinet. They must have been stronger than I thought.' She rubbed her eyes.

I snatched them out of her hand, peered at the label, and then blasted at her furiously, 'These were prescribed for Jack, for Christ's sake. He's a strapping six footer and you're only just over five, added to which, they're months out of date. You must know that you should *never* take medication prescribed for anyone else. Are you completely mad? You could have killed yourself.'

'I just wanted to get to sleep,' she said mildly, 'and I did – so no harm done. Anyway,' she glanced at the clock, 'what on earth were you thinking to leave me in bed until this time?'

I stared at her, unable to believe what I was hearing, and then I spun on my heel and marched out of the room, not trusting myself to speak.

I had the kettle on and the teacups out by the time Jack joined me.

'She's just getting showered and dressed,' he told me. 'She'll be down in a bit. I wouldn't be too hard on her, you know, Fay. I'm quite obviously the one to blame here.'

'Oh.' I glared at him and said bitterly, 'I'm only too well aware of exactly where to lay the blame for all of this. I don't need reminding of that fact, thank you very much, Jack.'

'We can't leave everything up in air like this, Fay. You must understand that. I came round because – as I said earlier – I

32

thought we should talk and at least try to sort things out.'

'Yes, I'm sure you did,' I agreed, making a huge effort to be civil and another effort to keep my tone pleasant and reasonable, 'but as far as I'm concerned, there is nothing to talk about and a cat in hell's chance of sorting anything out. You opted out of this marriage the minute you embarked on an extramarital affair and, if you're truthful, you would be saying the same thing to me should the shoe be on the other foot.'

'Ugh?' he grunted, as if I was speaking double Dutch.

'If I had been the one caught having an affair,' I explained patiently, 'you'd have divorced me so fast my head would be spinning, and,' I held my hand up as he attempted to interrupt me, 'please don't even bother to deny it. In the whole of our twenty years together, I don't recall either of us *ever* agreeing that ours would be an open marriage.'

'It was a stupid mistake, a lapse,' he began. 'You have to listen, Fay, let me explain. You owe me that much.'

'*I* owe *you*, Jack? I don't *think* so. I'm not interested in your explanations – in fact, I'm not interested in *you*, end of story. You're definitely not the man I thought you were.'

'So I make one mistake, and that's it?' He sounded offended.

'I wouldn't class an on-going affair as "one mistake", would you? No one buys expensive jewellery for someone who was little more than a one-night stand. In the scheme of things,' I glared at him, 'it was also a pretty big mistake and it is actually grounds for a divorce.'

'*Divorce*? No, Fay, you can't mean it.' For the second time that morning I watched his face lose its healthy colour, and knew he had finally begun to see there were consequences to his actions and that perhaps sorry wasn't going to be anywhere near enough.

'If it wasn't Boxing Day,' I stated flatly, 'I would be knocking on a solicitor's door right at this moment.'

'No,' he gasped, 'please don't do this, Fay. I love you – I've never stopped loving you.'

I shook my head. 'Spare me, Jack. You're wasting your breath. A man who loves his wife doesn't go screwing around. That's the action of a man who no longer gives a sh—'

My mother chose that moment to walk in, rolling up her sleeves and saying breezily, 'Shall I make a start on a meal? It can't be good to go without food, you know with the b—'

Thankfully, I realized just in time what she was about to say, and jumped in to say with a warning glare in her direction, 'Yes, I know it's a bit late for *the breakfast*,' I accentuated carefully, 'but maybe brunch. Jack was just leaving – weren't you, Jack?'

'Actually, no, I wasn't.' A belligerent look came over his face. 'You can't give up on our marriage just like that, Fay.'

'*I* didn't.' I met his gaze steadily. '*You* did.'

'But I didn't think—' he began.

'*That*,' I interrupted, 'is painfully obvious.'

'Look,' Mum stepped in, holding up her hands in an effort to cool things down, 'why don't the two of you go into the lounge and talk things over, and leave me to rustle up something to eat?'

If only to get him away from my mother and her thoughtless comments, I relented, and made my way to the door.

Jack quickly followed me, saying over his shoulder, 'A turkey sandwich would be nice, Iris.'

He didn't wait for her reply, and obviously didn't hear the 'fat chance,' I muttered under my breath, so when he walked into the lounge he stopped so abruptly that I cannoned into him, and he stared open-mouthed around a room devoid of any sign of the festive season we were still in the middle of, and demanded, 'What on earth happened to Christmas?'

'Well,' I replied sourly, 'I think you should know the answer to that better than anyone else, Jack. I threw it in the dustbin – along with all my hopes and dreams for the future. So I wouldn't pin your hopes on getting that turkey sandwich any time soon if I were you.'

He sank into an armchair, the same one I had hidden his tiny Christmas gift in, and it was clear to see the far-reaching repercussions of his behaviour were finally beginning to sink in. In fact, I thought he looked so ill that the sharp retort not to make himself at home remained unspoken on my lips.

'Please, Fay, don't do this to me – to us. I have no excuse. It should never have happened. It meant nothing and I've behaved like a complete idiot. I really am more sorry than I can ever say. Nothing like it has ever happened before and nothing like it will ever happen again. I will do anything – and I do mean *anything* – if you will give me a chance to make this up to you.'

'I wish it were as easy as that.'

'It is,' he began, his expression earnest.

'*Not*,' I finished for him with heavy emphasis. Then I added, 'You might be able to put this behind you, Jack, but I'm afraid I can't say the same. It's a shame that you felt able to risk everything we had for something that "meant nothing". Our relationship has always been built on trust and now that trust is completely and utterly gone. Do you really think I can ever be in your arms again without imagining you with *her*?'

Jack's shoulders slumped. He was the very picture of dejection and I even had it in me to feel sorry for him – but only for a moment – then I hardened my heart, reminding myself that he had made his choices and now it was time for me to make mine.

I would have preferred for him to leave right away, but my mother came in – as if on cue – to advise us that the meal was ready and we should eat it while it was hot. Jack didn't say a word when he was faced with a steaming plate of beans on toast, but sat down and tucked in with every appearance of enjoyment. He even made an effort at general conversation, but to say it was stilted was a massive understatement.

'Jack could give you a lift home, Mum,' I suggested eventually, 'it will save me getting the car out.'

They both stared at me, a startled expression on each face.

'I don't like to think of you here all alone,' my mother protested, 'you know, what with—'

'What with all that's happened,' I hastily finished the sentence for her, frowning at her ferociously and wondering if I could really trust her not to blurt out the news of a pregnancy that I was nowhere near ready to share with my deceiving husband.

Then she smiled a secret apology and I had no choice but to accept that she would be making a much bigger effort, at least until I was ready. I knew I really didn't have much option but to trust her not to let me down, whatever her own views were on the matter.

'I need some time alone to think about where I go from here,' I told them both, 'and I will have to start getting used to living alone eventually, too – but not here, of course.' I turned to Jack. 'The house will have to be put on the market as soon as possible.'

'No.' He looked dumbstruck. 'There's no need for that, Fay, really, there is no need.'

'There's every need.' I pointed out. 'You're entitled to half and now that we're separating, we'll need a residence each – unless you're intending to move in with your mistress.'

'She's not—' Jack protested.

I gave him a look. 'Not what, Jack, your mistress? What would you call her? Unless I'm very much mistaken, someone – other than your wife – with whom you are having a sexual relationship, is classed as a mistress.'

'I wouldn't call her anything, because as I've already told you, it's over,' he said, as if that made everything all right.

'Oh, Jack,' my mother suddenly burst out as if she could contain her comments no longer, 'it shouldn't have even started. What were you thinking, to throw everything away for a – a – *fling*? That's so not like you. I have to say I thought better of you.'

'She pursued me – made it almost impossible for me to say no.'

'Spare us the details and the excuses, please,' I spat, and continued, suddenly desperate to see the back of the pair of them. 'If you two want to discuss this tawdry business in any detail, then please feel free, but would you mind doing it elsewhere – preferably after you've left. Oh and Jack, please take your things with you when you go.'

Marching into the hall, I made sure Jack had followed before I opened the cloakroom door and indicated the heap of bulging black bags piled inside. Jack looked shocked all over again but, without a word of protest, he loaded them two at a time into his car, after which they finally left – with assurances from my mother that she would be back, and from Jack a promise that this wasn't over, that he wouldn't let it be. He gathered that I was very angry – as I was entitled to be – and he was only giving me time to reflect.

I slumped back against the front door and let the blessed

silence of the house surround me for a moment, before making another more meticulous tour of the house, collecting up the odd book, CD, tie and even a pen belonging to Jack. I wasn't happy until just about every trace of him was removed – and then I turned my attention to the photographs.

The most recent were large ones and on canvas from recent holidays in Egypt, Morocco, the States and Australia. We looked so happy – despite the fact those holidays had been taken as a kind of consolation because it had seemed increasingly unlikely that the family we'd always yearned for would ever become a reality.

After trying for a baby for the majority of almost twenty years of marriage, during which there were numerous false alarms and heartbreaking miscarriages, we had finally made the choice to give up on the fertility charts and hospital appointments and just get on with our lives. We still had each other, and that was enough, or that's what I had thought but, apparently, I hadn't been enough for Jack, after all.

Furious to realize I was crying, I wrenched our smiling likenesses from the walls and taking them outside with a bundle of newspapers I set fire to them in the middle of the back lawn. The ones in frames behind glass would simply have to be consigned to the dustbin, I decided as I watched the flames take hold and our smiling faces begin to char.

Becoming conscious that I was holding one such frame, I looked down at it in surprise. I had no recollection of lifting the black and white wedding photograph from the sideboard and now I glared at it in dislike, hating our smugly satisfied expressions, and then hurled it with great force across the garden. I could feel only satisfaction when it smashed to pieces against the wide trunk of a horse chestnut tree.

'Shot,' I muttered under my breath, and using the toe of

my shoe poked a canvas that had so far escaped the flames unscathed until it was deep into the burning embers of my impromptu bonfire.

'Who's there? What's going on?'

I whipped around at the sound of a quavering voice from the other side of the hedge and swore under my breath.

'It's only me, Mrs Bramshaw. Just burning a bit of rubbish, I'm sorry if I disturbed you.'

Her voice, sounding stronger, advised me, 'It is an offence, you know, to burn household waste and cause pollution or harm people's health. You can also be fined if you light a fire and allow the smoke to drift across the road and become a danger to traffic.'

She sounded as if she knew what she was talking about and had probably studied every by-law on the subject in minute detail, waiting for an opportunity such as this to present itself in order to air her knowledge.

'Oh, right,' I said, trying to sound suitably chastened and contrite. 'Well, I'm sorry, but there isn't much smoke and it is almost out now.' I poked another canvas deeper into the flames.

'I also heard the sound of breaking glass,' she sounded accusing now, but I thought she might well have feared that a break-in was taking place, so I made an effort to be understanding.

'Yes, sorry again. I tripped and broke the tumbler of water I was carrying. I'll be going back indoors as soon as the flames are out and I promise not to disturb you again tonight. I apologize if I worried you.'

The shock of her head, in a brown knitted bobble hat, suddenly appearing above the hedge made me jump almost out of my skin, even though I had known she was there.

'I really wouldn't attempt to burn the tree if I was you,' she cautioned quite kindly, 'it would probably make an awful lot of smoke, you know, with it still being green.'

I looked at her stupidly for a moment before I grasped she was referring to the discarded Christmas tree, and wandered over to assure her face to face that I wasn't thinking of doing any such thing.

She nodded, peering at me through the longer strands of foliage at the top of the hedge and suddenly asked, 'Have you been crying, dear?'

I rubbed quickly at my wet cheeks and denied firmly, 'Oh no, it was just the smoke, the wind blew it into my eyes.'

'Oh,' she said, and then shocked me by adding, 'only I know it's not uncommon to be very emotional when you're pregnant, bursting into tears all over the place at the drop of a hat and for no good reason.'

'How did you...? Only no one else knows yet apart from the obvious people in the medical profession – well, only my mother, and only just.'

'How did I know? Why, I used to be a midwife, dear, and can often recognize the signs even from a distance. Did I never tell you that?'

She hadn't, which was hardly surprising since I scarcely ever gave her the time of day despite having lived next door for so long, though I recalled that I'd often poked fun of Jack for what I'd called 'gossiping over the fence' with our elderly neighbour.

The thought that she might inadvertently inform Jack of my condition made me suddenly say, 'Could I possibly come round and talk to you for a moment, Mrs Bramshaw?'

Bless her, she was so transparently thrilled to have a visitor, bustling round her immaculate, if old-fashioned kitchen, setting the ancient aluminium kettle onto the gas hob and arranging bone china cups and saucers covered in roses onto a tray with pictures devoted to celebrating one of the Queen's jubilees. Watching her fill a little milk judge and add a proper sugar bowl with a lid, I felt as if I'd stepped back in time.

The tea was hot and fragrant, made from the loose leaves that so few people bothered with any more, and then poured through a strainer. However, the biscuit she offered was so stale that there was no crunch left in it, but I ate it anyway, not wanting to offend her. Something that smelt delicious was simmering on the hob, though, and my stomach growled.

My neighbour was one of those people whose age was difficult to guess. With her grey hair scraped back into a bun and wearing an old-fashioned floral pinafore that didn't flatter her long thin frame, it was clear that her appearance was of no importance to her, but she seemed very kind. I watched her pour more tea and her grip on the handle was firm.

I wasn't sure how to go about requesting that she didn't share the news of my pregnancy with my husband – the baby's own father – so in the end I just told her the truth about everything that had happened the previous day. I also shared our history of unsuccessful pregnancies and the shock of discovering that I was pregnant again at my age.

I went on to explain that I had originally only intended to keep the news of the pregnancy secret from Jack until I felt more certain that it would be viable and result in a live baby – unlike all of our other heartbreaking experiences. She made it surprisingly easy to talk, sitting quietly with her hands folded on her pinafored lap, asking no questions and making no comment until I had finished the whole sorry tale.

Then she simply said, 'Oh, my dear,' and passed me a spotlessly clean, lace-edged handkerchief when I burst into tears.

She didn't have to say any more because I just knew my secret would be safe with her. I very much doubted I was the only pregnant woman being cheated on by her husband that she had come across in her years as a midwife. She even agreed when I said as much.

'But most, I have to say,' she added, 'found forgiveness in their hearts and gave their man a second chance – even a third chance in some cases.'

'There you are, then,' I said, pulling a face, 'when they've done it once and got away with it, the chances are they will do it again. This is killing me – I cannot and will not go through it again. To be honest, it's only the thought of the baby that's keeping me going. If anything went wrong now ...'

'How far along are you, dear?' Betty asked – we were on first name terms by this time. 'Only if you've had your twelve week scan – yes, I am up to date with most of today's technology – you will already know that the pregnancy has passed the most delicate period.'

'I'm eighteen weeks,' I admitted a little sheepishly. 'I honestly didn't intentionally keep my pregnancy secret for so long. Only, you see, when I went for my first scan it showed that I was further along than I thought, and by then it was so close to Christmas that I thought the bootees wrapped in Christmas paper would be the perfect way of breaking the news to Jack.' I sniffed and a single tear rolled down my face.

Betty didn't say anything – well, there was nothing much she could say, really – but she patted my hand and proffered another clean hanky.

'So, you think this little mite,' I covered the slight swell of my belly with both hands in a gesture of protection, 'should have a good chance of making it to full term?'

'Almost halfway, dear, I would say there's every chance of

the safe arrival of a bonny early summer baby. However,' she added on a strong note of caution, 'stress isn't good during pregnancy and the break-up of a marriage is one of the most stressful things that can happen in a person's life, you know. So you must take great care.'

Part of me already knew that and I saw that subconsciously it might have had a lot to do with my determination to remain calm when Jack's affair had come to light in such a cruel and unexpected way.

Well, I might have lost everything else, but I was determined to do everything I could to keep this baby safe. I *would* have the family I had always dreamed of – with or without Jack in my life.

'I will,' I assured her, and rising to my feet, said, 'I must go, I've taken up enough of your time.'

I turned to leave but, before I could take a step, dizziness swept over me and, as everything turned black and I began to fall, I knew I was losing the baby and even as I lost consciousness, I was damning Jack to hell.

Chapter Four

As the blackness lifted and I slowly became aware of surroundings that were only very vaguely familiar, I was already crying; deep wrenching sobs that hurt my chest and left me gasping for breath. I opened my eyes slowly, then I closed them again quickly, reluctant to face the loss of the one precious thing that had been left in my life to make it worth living.

The room came into focus and I realized I was still in my elderly neighbour's kitchen. What I was doing there in her house, for the moment escaped me, but I was apparently lying on the floor and something soft had been placed under my head. She was leaning over me, her kindly face creased with concern.

'Oh, my dear, don't take on. I'm sure you just stood up too fast and the sudden movement caused you to faint. It's your condition, your hormones, and you probably haven't been eating properly – what with everything that's been going on – or you may even be anaemic.'

'The baby…?'

'I'm quite positive is fine,' she assured me, immediately taking the time to give me an efficient, if quick, once over. 'If you were bleeding heavily it would have soaked through your jeans by now, and you're not in any physical pain, are you? No, I thought not. Let me help you up.'

I struggled to my feet, using Betty's surprisingly sturdy arm, and the back of a chair for support – because my legs didn't seem to belong to me. Once I was seated again she hurried to put the kettle on, intent on making 'hot sweet tea, dear, for the shock you've had.' I made no demur because I still felt very shaken – in fact, I found I was extremely reluctant to face the thought of going home and having to manage without Betty's support and knowledge.

The bowl of stew that appeared in front of me in a very short time was surprisingly tasty, full of chunks of rich meat, sliced vegetables and fluffy dumplings in thick gravy. I cleared the bowl in no time and accepted a second helping. I must have been more hungry than I thought; obviously two rounds of beans on toast in two days wasn't anywhere near enough to sustain a pregnant woman. Never mind eating for two – I hadn't even been eating for one and was going to have to take more care.

'You're very kind,' I said, protesting, 'but I really shouldn't be eating your food.'

'You don't know what a pleasure it is to have someone to share a meal with, my dear.' Betty looked up from her own bowl. 'I enjoy cooking so much, I always have, but it's terribly tedious to eat every meal alone and I'm ashamed to say I usually have a tray on my lap at teatime and watch *The Chase* on television while I eat.'

'Well, this is absolutely delicious,' I told her truthfully. 'You must let me have the recipe.'

'Bless you,' she laughed then, a tinkling sound, 'there's no recipe. I make it the way my mother did by throwing in whatever I've got. Good lean meat, cooked thoroughly, seasonal vegetables and lots of stock.'

'And the dumplings,' I reminded her, 'don't forget the dumplings.'

She laughed again, and offered, 'I'll come over one day and show you – if you like.'

The latter was said hesitantly, and made me feel awful for the many times I'd thoughtlessly rebuffed her friendly overtures and been so quick to label her nothing more than a nosy old gossip.

'I would love that,' I hastened to say and opened my mouth again to suggest making a date – and then I suddenly fell silent and my spoon hovered between plate and mouth as my world shrank to a very odd sensation that I couldn't quite identify.

'What is it, dear?'

I had been staring into space for several minutes when Betty spoke, breaking my concentration, and I looked up to find her curious gaze resting on my face.

'I think,' I said slowly, 'that I felt something. It was most odd and I don't know if I can explain it.'

'The baby,' she suggested. 'Did you feel the baby move?'

'I'm not sure.' I knew I sounded vague. 'It felt like a fluttering, like a butterfly was trapped in there.' I rubbed a hand across my belly, but whatever it was had stopped.

'It *was* the baby,' she said, more definitely this time, 'I'm sure of it. We used to call it the quickening in my day and that could very well have had something to do with you fainting, too. I remember one of my patients sliding down her mother-in-law's sideboard when it happened to her – out cold for a minute or two, she was – just like you, Fay.'

'The baby *is* all right, though?' I knew I was fussing but I couldn't help it, I still felt extremely anxious.

'It's a very good sign that you can feel movement,' she assured me, 'and your twenty week scan is due soon, isn't it?'

I nodded. 'In two weeks.'

'Don't you think you should tell your husband before that, dear? In spite of what he's done, he is the baby's father and he really does have a right to know. You might think he's a terrible husband at the moment but that doesn't mean he won't be a good father.'

She looked nervous – as if she was waiting for me to bite her head off – but I didn't have the heart after all of her recent kindness to me – and anyway I knew she was right. My original reason for keeping the news from him was good. I hadn't told Jack in the first place because I wanted to be sure we had a reason to celebrate, I hadn't told him since the revelation of his affair because I wanted to punish him – to hurt him the way he had hurt me – but I accepted that I couldn't keep it from him forever.

'You're right, Betty. Of course you're right. This isn't just about me. I will tell Jack – before the scan – I promise. Now,' I rose to my feet, very carefully this time, 'I've taken up enough of your time and enjoyed your wonderful stew, but I really should be getting home.'

'I'll come with you, my dear.' She immediately came to stand beside me, her hand on my arm, but I shook my head. 'Just to the front gate then,' she tried for a compromise.

'I'll be fine, really.' I was turning towards her, smiling to show just how fine I was and then turned back to pull the kitchen door open, coming to an abrupt halt when I noticed there was a dog standing in front of me, blocking the way. It didn't look like a fierce dog, but it was quite a big one and I wasn't at all used to dogs of any kind.

'Oh.' I took an involuntary step back. 'You have a dog, Betty.'

'I actually have three,' she said, a smile in her voice, 'that one is Gemma. She's come looking for her supper. She won't hurt you – well, none of them will, but perhaps you don't like dogs?'

'I think I do, but I just don't know any.' I reached out a hand to smooth the sandy-coloured head of what looked like a Lurcher of some kind. 'Jack and I have even considered getting one at various times in the past but it wouldn't have been fair with us both working full time. I'm just amazed I've never heard yours barking. Where are the others?'

'Come and see,' she invited, and I followed her into a cosy sitting room. A TV burbled quietly in the corner – the flickering screen being watched intently by a pair of dogs curled in baskets placed either side of a brown corduroy sofa. The brindle dog did little more than look me up and down but the other, a border collie, came to greet me.

'That's Sadie still in the basket and this is Zoe. I went to the local rescue centre for one dog – for company, you know – and came home with three. Well, I was told they had come in together and they'd had such a bad time – brought in covered in sores and starving – that I didn't have the heart to separate them. I've had them five years and they've yet to make a sound.'

'They're beautiful.' I knelt down and the two dogs came to sit in front of me, the better for me to make a fuss of them, and eventually, Sadie made the effort to come and join them.

'Now that's unusual, she doesn't normally like to miss even a minute of her favourite programme.'

'Obviously doesn't want to be left out.'

The old lady and all three dogs came to the door to see me out. 'Now, are you sure you wouldn't like me to see you to your front door?'

I shook my head, stepping out onto the path. 'But thank you, Betty, for everything.'

I hadn't noticed a clock anywhere in the house next door, but it must have been later than I thought, because it was really quite dark outside and the street was completely deserted. I felt very alone when Betty closed her front door behind me. Everyone had someone to celebrate Boxing Day with, it seemed, even Betty had her dogs.

Glad of the security light when it came on as I set foot on the driveway, I made my way round the side of the house, noticing the faint glow still coming from the embers that were left of my spontaneous bonfire. Just as well I had instinctively lit it in the middle of the lawn and not near to the fence or the house. I hadn't given too much consideration to health and safety when I'd struck the first match.

Wandering over to take a closer look in case a well-aimed bucket of water might be a requirement, I felt the crunch of glass under my feet and recalled the furious throwing of the photo. I really should have given more thought to my actions and any repercussions, and I made a mental note to come out in the morning when I could see to clear it up.

Only as I walked through the back door did I realize how very tired and emotional I felt. Hardly surprising, really, I acknowledged, given all that had happened since only the day before.

Christmas Eve had seen me a happily married woman, buzzing with anticipation at the thought of breaking the spectacular news of an entirely unexpected but very welcome pregnancy to my husband. Wind forward just a little more than forty eight hours and my whole life lay in tatters, my marriage completely wrecked and my house stripped of all the things that had made it into a home – including my husband.

Though I couldn't wait to fall into bed, no sooner had I crawled under the duvet than my mind immediately came alive, leaping like a flea on a cat from one uncomfortable thought to the next. The distasteful to-do list came back to haunt me. Again it was headed, as I had told Jack it would be, by the necessity of finding a solicitor to act for me in the case of our divorce and contacting an estate agent about putting the house on the market.

It was all right for Jack to look horrified, to say there was no need, but he didn't know about the baby yet. Any divorce proceedings would need to include provisos regarding the child. Added to that, there was obviously no point in going to the expense of setting up a nursery in this house when the place would obviously have to be sold and the proceeds of the sale divided to enable us to buy our own homes.

I quailed at the thought. I was fast approaching forty but I had never lived alone, marrying straight from my parents' house – as most of us still did in those far off days. The very idea was daunting – even more daunting was the terrifying notion of being pregnant and alone, and facing life as a single mother with a brand new baby.

Anger flashed through me at the thought of the life I was being forced into, though I did my best to damp it down, ever determined as I was to protect the blameless child of this failed marriage. A child so deserving of the best start in life that I could give it – and that included protecting it from the harm that high levels of stress might cause.

How could I not be angry, though? If Jack hadn't been happy with our relationship, then why the hell hadn't he said something to me? That would have been the honest thing to do, surely? At least then I would have had some warning, some indication of what was to come. I couldn't believe the bloody man's duplicity. Did he really think that rushing off to bed with someone else was a reasonable solution to whatever he had decided was lacking in our marriage? Suddenly, I couldn't bear to be lying in the wide bed I had shared with Jack, and flinging back the duvet, I stumbled to my feet.

The house felt too big, too dark and too silent. While I couldn't do anything about the size of it, I could – and did – switch lights on everywhere I went, and turned radios and TVs on as I wandered from room to room. Looking for other things to do, I made tea that I didn't drink, toasted bread that I didn't eat and, finally, fell asleep on the three-seater sofa in the lounge, huddled into the warmth of my thick towelling robe.

I slept deeply, struggled back to consciousness at one point and became more than a little confused to find the lights and TV off, and what appeared to be the duvet from the bed covering me. I might have felt more concerned, but I was still so tired that it was easy to convince myself I must have done all of that while half asleep. Odd that the sun was streaming into the room as well, when I felt almost certain that the curtains had been pulled across the windows the night before, so I accepted that I must have done that, too.

Feeling no inclination to get up and rush around, I snuggled deeper into the cosiness of the quilt and must have dozed off again. When I woke some time later the central heating had come on to warm both the house and me, and I was wrapped tightly in my cocoon. In fact, I was so uncomfortably hot that I fought my way out of the depths of the duvet, and made my way through to the kitchen and straight out into the back garden.

Taking deep breaths of the cool morning air, I enjoyed the feel of it on my over-heated skin for a moment or two, but was soon pulling my robe tighter around me and pulling up the collar against the freezing December temperature before heading back to the house.

About to step inside, I turned around and stared across the lawn, and then turned again and walked slowly across the damp grass until I was looking down at the blackened area that was all that was left of the previous evening's bonfire. I'd have expected to see at the very least a pile of ashes, even charred pieces of canvas, but there was nothing but a black round of burned grass. Somehow, I wasn't then surprised to find that of the shards of glass and broken photo frame there was no sign.

It had to have been Betty, of course. The realization made me smile and wonder at her continuing kindness as I stepped back inside and closed the door behind me. She obviously hadn't wanted me to wake to that mess and the reawakened memories of what had set me off on that particular path of destruction. I reached out to switch on the kettle and finding it unmistakeably warm, I pulled my hand back and stood there staring at it, feeling the first trickle of real unease along my spine.

It could all have been Betty. Either that or I was going mad and doing all kinds of things that I couldn't remember doing. I stared at the kettle and then found myself staring at the back door and trying to recall whether or not I'd had to unlock it before I could step outside. If it wasn't Betty, than who the devil else would have walked into my house and started setting things to right – and why?

The answer whooshed into my head with all the fury of an exocet missile and every trace of fear disappeared instantly. I stormed into the hall.

'All right,' I shouted at the top of my voice, 'you've been rumbled so you can come out now.'

I'd been expecting Jack, of course, but when a sound made

me turn and look up, to my complete amazement I found myself looking at a complete stranger – a woman – standing at the top of the stairs.

For a long moment I could only stare up at her, completely lost for words until, making a gargantuan effort I was able to demand, 'And just who the bloody hell are *you* and what are you doing in *my* house?'

She seemed so absolutely unperturbed about being caught somewhere she obviously had no business to be, that I felt totally wrong-footed myself and could only watch as she sauntered down the stairs as if she owned the place. When she was standing in front of me, we took stock of one another and strangely I wasn't afraid or even very angry – just very, very curious. Perhaps because she was a woman I didn't feel any sense of danger.

Her hair was that dense shade of blue-black and it hung long and gleaming over her shoulders and down her back. Possibly in her late forties, I decided, though very well-preserved, she was dressed to kill – but not in a murderous way – in a long cream wool coat teamed with black accessories. The woman was slim and tall, the height of the stiletto heeled shoes on her feet adding unnecessary inches to her stature. She was very attractive indeed – flawless make-up accentuated her wide grey eyes and full lips – and she was obviously someone who was well aware of her own good looks.

She stared down at me and I tried – and failed – not to feel intimidated by either her height or her undoubted beauty.

Drawing my robe tightly around me, I asked again, in a very civil tone, 'Who are you? And what are you doing in my house?'

She smiled, the red lips parting to display perfect white teeth. The smile didn't reach her eyes, which were cold with the hint of steel about them, and up close the illusion of youth gave way to the unnatural tautness that was achieved only by Botox, surgery or both.

'I was curious about you, Fay, and can you blame me?' She suddenly caught sight of herself in the hall mirror and visibly preened. 'Hardly competition, are you? I've never seen such complacence in any woman. Slobbing round in a—' she wrinkled her straight nose in distaste, '—bath robe.' She couldn't have sounded more disparaging if I'd been wearing a horse blanket. 'And at *this* time of day, and with the house looking as if a tornado has hit it.'

Ignoring the sight of a duvet half on the couch and half on the floor in the lounge, and the thought of the unmade bed upstairs, I demanded, 'And that would be any of your concern because...?' Before the words were even completely out of my mouth, I suddenly knew the answer, and a swift intake of breath made me so dizzy that it was all I could do to remain on my feet. '*You*,' I said, my tone flat and angry, 'how did you get in here, and what the hell do you want? You have absolutely no business—'

'I have every business,' she said, her cool tone suddenly savage. 'He was already mine – *mine* – do you hear?' She took a step towards me and I took a hurried step away. 'He was ready to leave you – and no wonder. Just look at yourself. I have *nothing* to fear from the likes of you.'

It was all becoming crystal clear to me. There could be no doubt exactly who this woman was and what she wanted with me. Jack really had finished with her then, but had obviously neglected to tell her I had already thrown him out. Part of me longed to tell her she could have him, but another, more vindictive part wouldn't give her the satisfaction of knowing the havoc she had wrought in our marriage.

'So you say,' I taunted, 'but he's not with *you*, is he? If he was, you wouldn't be here. Women like you make me sick, nothing is sacred, is it? Any man in trousers is fair game.'

'At least women like me are interested in what's inside those trousers and in sending a man to work with a huge smile on his face. Smug women like you think a wedding ring really is all it takes to keep a man by your side, that and the promise of sex on Saturday nights – when you can be bothered. I looked in your underwear drawer, Fay, and I can tell you that boring white cotton really is *not* the way to turn a man on.'

'There's actually more to life and love than red basques and black stockings,' I said coldly, wondering at my ability to stand there and fight my corner when it was quite clear I was at a serious disadvantage, despite the fact I was standing in my own house.

'If that's what Jack told you, then he is lying through those lovely white teeth of his.' She smiled then, not so much like a cat who'd got the cream, more like a python swallowing its prey. 'From my experience, black and red are his favourite colours.'

'Are they, though?' I forced myself to smirk. 'Or is it a case of too much of a good thing? Too rich a diet can pall very quickly, you know.'

She looked me up and down very, very slowly, her expression insolent. 'And man,' she said, 'especially a man like Jack – cannot live by bread alone – especially cheap white bread like you. I can give Jack the life he deserves – remind me now – what exactly is it that you can give him?'

'A *baby*,' I spat, suddenly losing it and throwing my trump card into the fray. 'I can give Jack the child he has always wanted – can you?'

A startled gasp had us both spinning round to face the door

we hadn't even heard open. Jack was standing there, but for how long he'd been there was anybody's guess. However, I didn't have to guess that he had heard my brief but unmistakeable and very clear declaration – whether or not he believed it was another matter.

'What the hell...?' Jack began furiously, and I waited for him to demand to know what I was talking about, trying to decide in a hurry whether the truth was in order at this point or a big fat white lie.

'What the hell,' he began again, 'are you doing here, Iona? And why,' he turned on me, 'did you let her in?'

'Because I wanted a cosy chat with your mistress, of course, Jack.' My tone was scathing. 'What do *you* think? You should be asking *her* how she got in, because I can assure you she certainly wasn't invited into the house by me. I discovered her making a leisurely tour of the house and she's quite happily admitted to going through my things.'

For a moment he looked startled and the next absolutely livid; thrusting out a hand, he demanded harshly, 'The key, Iona, you actually helped yourself to the key. I can't believe it. Give it to me – right now. No wonder I couldn't find it. How bloody *dare* you?'

'You can't say it's over, just like that, and assume that I'll simply accept it. What did you expect me to do, Jack – disappear with my tail between my legs, never to be seen again?'

'Actually, yes, I did. Where's your self-respect?'

'*My* self-respect, Jack? Where the hell is *yours*?' The woman, Iona apparently, drew herself up to her full, impressive height, and waving a dismissive hand in my dishevelled direction, ordered him, 'Look at her, go on, have a good look – and then look at me. There's no comparison, is there?'

'She has a point, Jack, doesn't she?' I shrugged, feeling I

had no choice but to be honest.

'No, she doesn't,' he denied emphatically, and I warmed a tiny fraction towards him, until he added, 'no one looks their best the minute they step out of bed and this isn't a competition. The key, Iona, and if you ever bother my wife again and I get to hear of it, I will be contacting the police.'

Iona's scarlet-tipped fingers dipped into the pocket of her coat, and withdrew the Yale key with Jack's BMW key ring still attached. She held it out between her thumb and first finger and, when Jack put out his hand for it, dropped it very deliberately on the floor at his feet before sauntering to the front door, as if she had all the time in the world.

She stopped with her hand on the latch, turned, and asked Jack with a look that should have shrivelled him up on the spot, 'Before I go, would you mind explaining to me how exactly your wife managed to get pregnant when you were very clear about the fact that your sex life was dead in the water? Immaculate conception, was it?'

Chapter Five

THE QUIET CLOSING of the front door behind Iona was obviously the final insult that let us know, loud and clear, that she thought neither one of us was worth the effort of a slam.

The jibe about our supposedly non-existent sex life had clearly hit home because Jack's complexion went from an interesting shade of purple to an insipid grey tinge.

'I didn't ...' he began and then hesitated. 'I wouldn't ...' He started again and then hurried on. 'I wouldn't talk about our sex life to *anyone*, least of all *her*. I really wouldn't, Fay.' But as he had bent down to pick up the dropped key at this point, I couldn't see his face, and he didn't have to meet my eye. It would have made no difference because I still knew without a shadow of a doubt that he was lying through his teeth.

'It doesn't matter,' I told him tonelessly and, when he protested, I repeated but firmly this time, 'I said it doesn't matter.'

'I'm so sorry, Fay. I'm really sorry.' This time Jack did look at me. He didn't actually say what exactly he was so sorry for, but that really didn't matter at all to me, either.

I shrugged to show my complete indifference.

'Can we talk?' His tone this time was pleading. 'This time

without your mother's well-meaning, but mostly unhelpful input,' and he added a, '*please?*' that was emphasized.

I didn't feel I had a choice, especially now he knew about the baby. I confess I was quite surprised that he wasn't firing questions in rapid succession at me about that already.

'All right,' I said, and saw his shoulders slump and the relief that showed on his face before he gathered himself together.

'Thank you.'

'Just give me time to shower and get ready for the day – after all, as you so rightly said earlier, "no one looks their best the minute they step out of bed", do they?'

Watching his discomfort and the hot colour that suffused his face once more gave me some kind of satisfaction. I went upstairs, dragging the duvet behind me, pausing only to advise him over my shoulder, 'You might want to make tea and perhaps find something for us to eat. It might have to be beans on toast again – I think that's about all the shop my mother went to could have had in stock. As a matter of fact, you can make yourself at home – but only just for now, of course. I won't be long.'

I took my time, making the bed, making up my face, straightening my hair and dressing as if I was going out to lunch. Jack was right, it wasn't a competition but I still had my pride.

I started making my way downstairs just as he came to the bottom of the stairs to call me. He paused there, looking up at me, and I couldn't pretend that the admiration I saw in his eyes didn't matter to me – even after everything that had happened.

We ate in silence. Jack hadn't burned the beans or the toast, but I couldn't help thinking longingly of Betty's tasty stew which had been a veritable feast by comparison.

'Is it all right?' he asked, when it must have become obvious to him that I didn't intend to make small talk.

'It's fine.'

He finished eating and pushed his plate away. 'I'm sorry, Fay, sorrier than I can say about – about – everything. I realize that I've ruined a lot more than Christmas.'

'It's fine,' I said automatically.

Jack looked at me as if I had gone completely mad.

'It's *fine*?' he burst out in the end, and then repeated, 'It's *fine* – how can you say that, when it clearly isn't bloody fine at all?'

I pushed away my own plate, with the beans in their gloopy sauce congealing unappetizingly on it, as if I was discarding the food because of his outburst, and not because I just couldn't face another bean, which was the real reason. I was actually still quite hungry.

'It is,' I said without expression, 'what it is. You clearly haven't been happy in this marriage for some time, Jack, and I'm glad to have finally been made aware of the fact – even if it was in a highly unconventional way. If you hadn't given the game away by mixing the Christmas gifts up in that clumsy way, when were you going to tell me – if ever?'

He clearly didn't know how to answer me, and floundered about like a fish out of water with his mouth opening as if he was about to say something, and then closing again as he thought better of it. I found it fascinating watching the husband I had never known to be lost for words to be – well – so completely and utterly lost for words.

'Cat got your tongue, Jack?' I asked, when I felt he had struggled long enough.

'There's nothing I can say or do, is there?' he said it almost accusingly. 'You know that. I'm totally in the wrong, and I hold my hands up.' I watched as he actually did hold his hands up and thought how foolish he looked. 'I can only apologize, over and over, and I will, for behaving like a total bloody arse, for being stupid enough to be led into an affair I didn't ever want, with a woman I don't actually like very much at all.'

'So,' I said in an interested voice, 'you're saying this is all what's-her-name's fault? Ah, yes, Iona, isn't it? What a very unusual name. She led you astray, did she?'

'Well, yes,' he told me earnestly, 'actually, she did. I told her I was happily married but she just wouldn't leave me alone. Phone calls, texts, emails – she even sent photos.'

'And you couldn't help yourself? Is that it, Jack?' I smiled sweetly, kindly almost.

Probably encouraged by what he took as my sudden understanding of the situation, Jack leapt to his feet and began an impassioned speech, pacing backwards and forwards as the words streamed from him.

'That's it,' he agreed, 'yes, that's exactly it, Fay. She wouldn't take no for an answer. Everywhere I turned, she was there. Everyone at work thought there was something going on long before there actually was just because she was always coming by my office, joining me for lunch without an invitation, turning up at the pub when I met the guys for a drink after work.'

'Oh, she *works* with you, does she?' I didn't really need to ask the question at all because I already knew the answer from the information being so hurriedly divulged.

'She's my *boss*,' he declared, as if I should have known, 'so you can see how difficult it was for me.'

'You couldn't say no to embarking on an affair with her because she was your boss?' I hazarded a guess that didn't make any sense at all to me, though it obviously did to Jack, because he pounced on words that were meant to be sarcastic, almost with glee.

'*Exactly*.' He looked – vindicated was the only word that came to mind. 'I knew you would understand, once you heard the facts.'

'So,' I hazarded another guess, '*you* would understand if I was having an affair with Peter Lucas?'

'Yes,' he said immediately, and quite clearly without thinking, and then, obviously having had time for second thoughts, hurriedly contradicted himself with a firm, 'no.'

'Which is it, Jack? Yes, you would understand if I had an affair with Peter, or no, you wouldn't?' I must admit it was fascinating as I watched him squirming like a butterfly pinned to a board. 'Peter is just as much my boss as Iona is yours, so that must make it all right, given that the same rules obviously apply, wouldn't you say?'

'I – urm – I … Damn it, it's not the same at all. You've known Peter for years – he's a friend. Jesus, Fay, I thought you would understand.'

'Oh, I am trying, really I am.' I nodded in what I thought was a very understanding way, and went on. 'So if a new boss came in, a stranger, six feet tall, like Iona, and very attractive, like Iona, *then* it would be OK for me to have an affair with him?'

'*No*.'

'That's the correct answer, Jack,' I said, pleased that he was beginning to understand where I was coming from, 'and I'm surprised it's taken you so long to realize that. It is never – I repeat, *never* - all right for a married man or woman to have an affair under *any* circumstances – unless …' I put my hand up to silence him as he went to interrupt. 'Unless the marriage is already dead in the water and both parties are aware of the fact. Now, are you beginning to understand my point of view and perhaps getting a little bit closer to taking total responsibility for your own actions?'

Jack's shoulders slumped. 'There was really no excuse for what I did, was there? And you're right, I wouldn't have been able to forgive you, not easily, had you done the same. But,' he added, 'I hope that I would at least have made an effort to try.'

'I'm nowhere near ready to even consider giving one single thought to forgiveness,' I said, being as honest as I could be, 'or to finding it at all easy to be around you – but I don't want us to be fighting all the time either. I appreciate that won't get us anywhere.'

'Just promise me that you won't do anything rash,' he pleaded. 'I put my hands up to the fact that I've behaved like a total shit, but you have always said that everyone deserves a second chance.'

'Did I really say that?' I wondered at how glibly the words must have been spoken. 'I suppose it's easy to behave generously before your generosity is really put to the test. You really ought to leave me in peace to think about where I go from here. I'm not sure why you keep turning up, Jack. It's really not helping.'

'Because I'm worried about you,' he said simply. 'How do you think I felt driving by in the early hours to see all the lights blazing and then, coming in to check you were all right? I found TVs on everywhere as well.'

'You were here – in the house?'

He nodded.

'So it was you who...?'

'Covered you with the duvet, turned off the lights and the radios and TVs? Yes, it was me. I couldn't just drive by, could I? Anything could have been happening in here.'

'But how did you get in when what's-her-name had, apparently, taken your key?'

'Through the back door – it was unlocked. Looks as if you had quite a bonfire out there.' He grimaced and shook his head. 'Are there any pictures of us left at all?'

I shook my head. 'No, not on the walls, though I haven't actually started on the albums yet.' I gave him a straight look and then demanded, 'Do you blame me, Jack?'

'It seems a bit harsh, but no, I don't really blame you. How could I? I don't blame you for giving her the impression you were pregnant, either. I heard some of what she was saying and I can quite understand that you were being severely provoked.'

There it was, the moment I had been dreading, the moment when the right thing to do would be to tell the truth, but he had given me the perfect excuse not to by thinking I would actually lie about such a thing.

'That's very understanding of you,' I found myself saying, but not confirming or denying the truth of the bold statement he had overheard. To be honest, I still didn't feel ready to share the truth with him. It would be like giving him a valued prize that he seriously did not deserve.

'Perhaps if we'd had children …' he began.

'Don't,' I turned on him furiously, knowing that telling him now was the last thing, the very last thing I would be doing. 'Don't you *dare* use the fact we don't have children as an excuse for the fact you chose to go off and start a tawdry little affair. Just go, Jack, just bugger off.'

'I'm sorry, I'm sorry.'

'Oh, believe me, Jack,' I said nastily and with feeling, 'you bloody well will be.'

'And believe *me*.' For the first time since this whole thing started, Jack actually turned on me. 'I couldn't possibly be any sorrier than I already am, but I have no bloody idea how to make you understand that I would give absolutely *everything* – and I do mean everything – that I own to be able to turn the time back to before this all happened.

'OK,' he said, as I rose to my feet, 'don't bother to get up. I'm going – but before I do, just let me say that I will do anything to try and put right what I have done wrong. I love you.' He saw the sneer I couldn't keep from my face, but he carried on regardless. 'I've always loved you and I always will. Whatever happens between us in the future, there will never be a day go by that I will not regret – with all my heart – how much I've hurt you.'

He took a step towards me and, thinking he was going to kiss me, I took a brisk step back and then had no idea why I should feel guilty when I saw how much my action had hurt him.

For the second time that morning, I listened to the front door being closed quietly and for the first time that morning I felt the baby move. I felt like bursting into tears, I felt like running after Jack, because this was his baby, too, and I still loved him. The trouble was that I also hated him and, just at the moment, it was easier to hate him than it was to love him.

I'd never been as relieved to return to work after a festive break, and never been so glad that, as Senior Programme Administrator at the popular Brankstone University, I had my own office. Applications being made though UCAS were still arriving thick and fast, especially now that the deadline was approaching, so my team of recruitment administrators had little time for the normal gossiping that took place after a break and would know that it was the same for me.

What with the short-listing of said applications, interviews to arrange – some of which would result in offers to be made and others for rejection letters to be sent – heads were down and everyone was concentrating on the job in hand every time I showed my face to collect printing or pass on information. I was busy myself with statistics and meetings which kept my mind occupied during the day – the evenings were another matter. Though I was often grateful for the company, I could certainly have done without either my mother or Betty looking askance at me every time I confessed that no, I hadn't yet told Jack about the baby, and always felt forced to add that I intended to do so soon.

When the twenty week scan loomed ever larger on my calendar, I knew I really should be putting off the moment no longer. Several times I even lifted the phone to make the call, before thinking better of it and replacing the receiver. In the end, though, I had left work and was actually on my way to the hospital to keep the appointment, when a sudden change of heart made me head to Jack's office to issue a very last minute invitation to join me in viewing the ultrasound scan of a baby he had no idea existed.

Jack had been strangely silent since our last meeting. Part of me was angry that he wasn't making more of an effort to stay in touch, while the other – more sensible part – reminded me that I would have given him short shrift if he had, and accused him of pestering me into the bargain.

Perhaps the fact that he wasn't on my case was the reason I hadn't carried out my threat to see a solicitor immediately after Christmas regarding a divorce, and neither had I rushed to put the house on the market. I could discuss those things with Jack once I had told him about the baby and then he would see the urgency of getting things sorted out.

There was no doubt that I missed him, in spite of

everything. You can't be married and close to someone for so many years without acknowledging the gap left when they were no longer around. I had a far clearer understanding now of what my mother had been through – the circumstances were quite different and yet there were definitely similarities – an abrupt end to married life for one thing and a gaping hole left in your life for another.

I'd pulled up outside of the tall building that housed Jack's office, and was sitting there trying to decide whether to go inside and find him or send a text when I spotted them.

Standing at the top of the steps leading down from the glass front doors, they made a striking couple. Both so tall and good looking, and Jack being so fair he was a perfect foil for Iona's dark beauty. They didn't seem to be in any hurry to make a move and I didn't have the time to hang around to see if they were going off together or separately. I told myself that I didn't care what their plans were but I was probably lying.

In the end, I threw the car door open, practically leapt from the vehicle and took the steps two at a time.

'When you've finished your cosy chat with *her*,' I spat into Jack's startled face, 'you might be interested to come and attend our baby's ultrasound scan – but please don't put your-self out, it's of little odds to me whether you do or not.'

With that I spun around and dashed away from the pair of them – and found myself stepping straight into thin air. It seemed forever before I landed in a crumpled heap at the bottom of the flight of steps. I lay for a moment, trying to decide which part of me hurt the most and then Jack was beside me, lifting me to my feet with infinite tenderness.

'Sweetheart, are you all right?'

Over his shoulder, still standing at the top of the steps, Iona stood as still as a statue and she didn't even bother to try and hide the smirk on her face as she stared down at me.

The baby, I thought. She assumed I was going to lose the baby – which had to be a distinct possibility after a fall like that. The realization that I had been irresponsible enough to lose my temper and in doing so had put my precious baby's life in danger was a devastating one. What on earth had I been thinking to allow myself to behave in such a reckless manner? And was I now going to pay the ultimate price?

'Get me to the hospital – now,' I screamed and Jack, to his credit, didn't hesitate but helped me into the passenger seat of my own car and taking the wheel, swerved out into the traffic, ignoring the furious tooting of horns.

I think, in his frantic state, had there not been a parking slot immediately available in the Maternity Unit car park, Jack would have parked anywhere. He commandeered a wheelchair from somewhere and rushed me inside so fast my head was spinning.

I don't know what he said to the receptionist but, before I knew it, I was being given a cursory examination and prepared for the ultrasound scan with Jack by my side. He looked shell-shocked, I thought, and very anxious. He held my hand so tightly that it hurt and said not a single word.

Even as the gel was being applied to the swell of my belly, I could feel the baby moving and this was confirmed when the image popped up on the screen. A little hand clearly waved, as if in greeting.

Jack burst into tears. 'It's a baby,' he whispered.

Chapter Six

ALL I COULD think about as we drove home in silence was the confused look the midwife gave Jack when he had uttered the words, 'It's a *baby*,' in such shocked tones. She was obviously wondering just exactly what he'd been expecting to see at a twenty-week antenatal ultrasound scan, when it was obvious we were together and even wearing matching wedding rings.

Not until I was tucked up on the couch with a cup of the hot, sweet tea I was getting a taste for by my side, did Jack ask the question that must have been eating him up inside.

'When exactly were you planning on telling me that I'm about to become a father? I'm assuming it's my baby – no, actually I *know* it's my baby – but twenty weeks, Fay – *twenty* bloody weeks without so much as a hint that you might be pregnant.'

'Just sit down, Jack, sit down and listen,' I ordered and, to his credit he did just that.

'For weeks,' I told him, 'I didn't even realize I was pregnant. Why would I, Jack? You know we'd both given up on the possibility long ago and we've had far too many false alarms for me to get excited over a missed period. When I suspected that I actually might be, I did a pregnancy test or two – well, actually, it was more like nine or ten.' Even he managed a smile at that admission. 'And then I made an appointment with the doctor, who confirmed the pregnancy and booked me in for an ultrasound scan.

'I intended to tell you after what I thought would be the twelve-week scan – when I could be pretty certain that the pregnancy was going to be viable. We've had so many false alarms and disappointments over the years that I really didn't want to raise your hopes along with mine only for them to be dashed again.'

'I can understand that – I think.' He nodded, but he sounded grudging and I didn't altogether blame him – until I reminded myself that, if he hadn't been otherwise engaged, he might have noticed something was amiss, and I hardened my heart again.

'Anyway,' I continued, 'when I had the scan, it immediately became clear that I was further along with the pregnancy than the twelve weeks I'd been expecting to have confirmed. It was so close to Christmas by then that I decided to wait just a little bit longer. I'd wrapped a pair of bootees in festive wrapping paper and could hardly wait to see your face when you opened them. They were what I was sure would be the best Christmas present ever.'

I didn't say any more – I didn't have to because he knew why that gift was never received by him. Jack groaned deeply and sank his head into his hands.

I then continued. 'Obviously after *your* little surprise I didn't have the least inclination to share my news with you.' I shrugged, scowled at him and asked, 'Can you really blame me?'

'No, I don't blame you at all. The question now is, where do we go from here?'

I shook my head, looked at him sadly, and said honestly, 'I don't know, Jack, I really don't know.'

'We could start by dealing with the here and now.' He looked serious. 'You took a right tumble today and I'm not happy to leave you alone in the house. We're so lucky that the baby is safe.' He didn't add the words 'for now' but I knew those words were uppermost in both of our minds. 'You were also incredibly lucky not to break any bones, but you are going to be very bruised and sore and will need looking after. I would like to be the one doing the looking after, Fay, but I know I will have to accept it if you tell me that you would prefer your mother to come over instead.'

I don't quite know how I came to agree with him staying in the spare room 'for now'. It might have been his pitiful expression, the obvious eagerness to become involved with a pregnancy he still couldn't quite believe or even my own desire to be able to share this miracle with the only person in the world to whom it meant as much as it did to me.

'You'll have to fetch some things,' I said, reminding him without any hint of an apology. 'There's nothing of yours in the house.'

'I don't like to leave you here alone – not even for a short time,' Jack said again, looking anxious. 'I know everything appeared to be fine with the scan, but you never know, and with a track record like ours, we don't want to be taking any chances at all.'

'Betty might be happy to sit with me for a while,' I suggested, feeling just as concerned about staying alone. My whole body was already beginning to feel sore and bruised, but the safety of the baby was my only concern. I knew I'd be happier with someone who knew the score and Betty fitted the bill better than anyone else I knew.

He looked puzzled. 'Betty? Who's Betty?'

I laughed, even though I didn't feel that much like laughing. 'You always talked to our neighbour much more than I ever did, yet you don't even know her name.'

'Oh, you mean Mrs Bramshaw? She's a bit old, isn't she? What use would she be in a crisis?'

'More than you know, Mr Doubter,' I said a tad smugly. 'She used to be a midwife.'

'No?' he said. 'Who'd have thought it? I'll pop and ask her if she minds, shall I?'

'That would be great.' I nodded, and then as he went to leave, I called after him, 'Hurry up. Oh and tell her she'd be very welcome to bring the dogs round with her.'

'Dogs?' he parroted. 'How many does she have? I didn't even know she had one.'

He didn't wait for the answer but went off to knock on Betty's door and was back in minutes, hefting Betty's massive saucepan with his hands protected by oven gloves. I could smell the stew the minute he came through the door and my mouth immediately began to water copiously.

'I've just been given specific instructions to put this on a low heat,' he told me. 'I think it's a casserole or something. It smells amazing, doesn't it? Betty's on her way.'

And, sure enough, there she was, bustling in right behind him. She was carrying a covered basket and I was sure the aroma of fresh bread came into the room with her. Her dogs were close behind and after looking around, they settled rather hopefully in front of the unlit fireplace. The flick of a switch brought the gas powered flames to life in the grate and they instantly moved closer to settle with contented sighs, enjoying the warmth. When I turned on the TV – even with the sound right down – the blissful expressions on all three of their faces were a joy to behold.

If only life were that simple, I couldn't help thinking. Everything was evidently right with their world – their needs were very simple after all – but it was painfully obvious that it was going to take more than a couple of switches to make everything right with mine.

'I'll just get this sorted,' Betty advised, turning to urge Jack, 'well, don't just stand there – bring it through, young man, and then go and do whatever you have to. When you get back it will be ready to eat.'

'He knows then?' She nodded her head in the departing Jack's general direction, sitting down on the armchair opposite the sofa and bringing a piece of knitting out of her bag.

I told her about the whole sorry episode that had led to me being laid up with Jack in attendance.

'We're both worried about the baby,' I explained, 'though the hospital didn't seem all that concerned, said the scan was fine and to call my midwife if I was at all worried.'

'Well,' she said, 'in this day and age, from what I can gather, they seem to tend to just let nature take its course. Babies are pretty resilient and survive all manner of things, protected as they are in the womb, but in my day you would certainly have been prescribed bed rest to give the baby the best chance after a fall like that.'

'I'm all for old-fashioned advice,' I told her, 'and if it was good enough for mothers-to-be in your day, it's good enough for me.'

'Well, it won't hurt you to put your feet up,' she said comfortably, 'because it sounds as if you took quite a tumble and you'll certainly be full of aches and pains by the morning.'

Jack was back so quickly, I wondered if his belongings had been in his car ever since he'd removed them from the house.

He'd mentioned taking a taxi instead of driving my car – and on his return, I recognized the sound of the BMW's engine as he pulled into the drive. However, I decided it was none of my business where he'd been spending his time and refused to give the matter so much as another minute's thought.

Betty's stew was every bit as tasty this time around. We ate it from large bowls set on trays, accompanied with doorstep slices of freshly baked bread slathered thickly with real butter.

Once my tray had been removed I sat back with a contented sigh, stroking Gemma who had moved to sit close beside me with her smooth Lurcher's head on my lap. For the first time since Jack's shocking bombshell had been dropped on Christmas day I did feel at some kind of peace with the world. Obviously not the world I had known and taken for granted for so long – not with my marriage in tatters – but there was the miracle of a baby to look forward to, whatever happened to Jack and me.

There was an uncomfortable lull after Betty had left, especially as she had advised me to have a warm bath 'to bring out the bruising and help you to sleep'. It felt ridiculously inappropriate, not to mention far too intimate, to take myself off to have a bath with Jack in the house, and that uneasy feeling was an indication of how much things had changed between us.

In the past we had shared a bathroom without a thought, even shared a bath or a shower on many occasions, and yet now it didn't feel right even knowing that he would be on the other side of a locked and bolted door.

As if he had read my mind, Jack said, 'It's not making you feel awkward having me in the house, is it? Only, for the safety of you and the baby, we both know it's for the best that I'm here. You go and take your bath, Fay, I'll stay down here until

I know you're safely in bed.'

'Why should I feel awkward?' I asked huffily, getting stiffly to my feet and ignoring the hand he held out ready to assist me. 'If anyone should feel awkward it's you. I don't have a problem at all with you being in the house, as long as you keep your distance and completely understand that it's a temporary arrangement – not permanent or ever likely to be again.'

He stood helplessly, watching my slow progress across the room, and as I reached the door, he said, 'I know I deserve it, but you seem so hard, Fay, so unforgiving.'

'Can you really blame me?' I demanded shortly as I left the room. 'You've ruined what should have been the happiest time of my life.'

I couldn't recall the last time I'd had the luxury of a good long soak in the bath. My life was so busy that I almost always showered for quickness, and had quite forgotten how good it felt to slide into the water and let the liquid warmth enfold your body. How long I lay there, dozing a little and allowing the soothing heat to do its work, I had no idea, but suddenly without warning the door burst open and Jack stood there, staring down at me.

'What the bloody hell do you think you're doing?' I yelled, grabbing for the towel and struggling to sit up.

'I did call your name, and when there was no answer I panicked,' he muttered, his gaze glued to the burgeoning belly I tried ineffectively to hide. 'I thought – erm – you know, that you might have slipped and hit your head, fallen asleep ...' His voice trailed off.

'Well, thank you for your concern but, as you can see,' I said tartly, 'I'm absolutely fine so you can go now.'

He had already turned sheepishly for the door when I began my struggle to vacate the bath tub and very quickly discovered that, with my battered body and baby bump combined, it wasn't going to be at all easy.

Jack was through the door and was already closing it behind him when I forced myself to mutter through clenched teeth, 'Erm, I could actually use a hand here.'

Either he didn't hear me, or he didn't want to and I found myself in the unenviable position of having to plead quite loudly. 'Jack, could you give me a hand, please?'

The door opened wider, and little more than Jack's nose appeared in the crack. 'Did you say something?' he asked politely.

'You know I bloody well did,' I fumed, hovering between being furiously angry and just plain embarrassed. 'I'm stuck,' I admitted finally.

He tried, unsuccessfully, to appear as if he was taking the situation seriously. 'You're stuck?' he repeated, and when his face was presented into the room his lips were definitely twitching.

I didn't deign to state the obvious again, just gave him a filthy look, so that he relented immediately, clearly understanding that he was skating on very thin ice. We were only just on barely civil terms, even Jack could see this was no time to see the funny side of anything involving the two of us and any kind of situation that forced us into unwelcome intimacy.

He took my hands and pulled, but each time I thought we were getting somewhere my feet slipped on the bottom of the bath and I sat back down into the bath tub again in a hurry, sending a tidal wave of water slopping out over the sides. The towel I was trying in vain to hold onto was also sopping wet and so, very quickly, was Jack.

'I'll let the water out,' I said tersely, and then found I couldn't lean far enough forward to reach the plug so that Jack had to even do that for me.

I had never felt so helpless – or so foolish – in my life, especially when Jack had to step into the bath, place his hands under my arms and haul me to my feet in the most undignified way. To cap it all when I stepped out onto the floor, I fell heavily against Jack and finally lost my grip on the towel.

To his credit, he just held me steady until I had gained my balance and then, reaching for a dry towel from the rack, wrapped it snugly around me. He held me for a few more moments and I felt no urge to pull away but, instead, enjoyed the feeling of being held again, of those strong and familiar arms around me. In those moments I could almost allow myself to believe that Christmas day had never happened. Unfortunately, it had and as soon as I remembered that, the moment was gone and so was the enjoyment. I didn't have to remind myself that nothing would ever be the same again.

'Are you OK now?' he looked down at me.

I nodded, and then pulled a rueful face and murmured as I extricated myself from his arms, 'Just feeling a bit silly – fancy not being able to climb out of the bloody bath.'

'Part and parcel of being pregnant, I suspect, and I'm just really glad I was here.'

I wanted to say that I was glad, too, but it felt wrong under the circumstances, so instead I glanced around and said, 'It's a bit of a mess.'

'You go and get ready for bed,' he encouraged, 'and leave me to deal with this. I'll bring you a hot drink later.'

With the morning came a stiffness that seemed to affect every single part of my body and left me struggling even to get out of bed. It didn't take more than a second's thought to convince me that the soothing effects of a bath wouldn't be worth the struggle to get in and out of the tub and I opted for the en-suite shower instead.

There was also a certain noticeable stiffness between Jack and me – the awkwardness definitely more on my part than his, since he couldn't have done enough for me.

'I've phoned work for you,' he informed me when I finally hobbled downstairs and into the kitchen, to find tea and toast waiting for me. He'd even put a posy of snowdrops on the table, which was probably a nice thought though it seemed a bit over the top and smacked to me of him trying a bit too hard. 'I told them you took a bit of a tumble.'

'You didn't...?'

'Mention the pregnancy?' He shook his head. 'I guessed you hadn't said anything when your boss didn't ask if the baby was all right and, as they weren't surprised to hear from me, I took it they knew nothing about our marital problems, either.'

I nodded. 'I'll tell them when I go back to work. I'm becoming more and more certain that this little one,' I rubbed my belly with a soft smile, 'isn't going anywhere until the time is right. Any difficulties we're facing at home are nobody else's business.' Jack just nodded.

'Amazing, isn't it?' Jack said eventually, allowing himself a regretful smile, 'After all the great years we've had together, the longed-for pregnancy should happen now – just when I've managed to screw things up for us and our marriage big time.'

I wanted to agree, to get angry again, even to cry for what might have been, but there seemed no real point. Regrets weren't going to turn the clock back and give us another chance to share what should have been a perfect moment in a shared life. This was how things stood, we finally had the pregnancy we had always wanted – together with a broken marriage that had to be dealt with, whether we liked it or not.

When it became clear that I had nothing to add to his blunt

statement, Jack said, 'I'll have to go in to work later, but I've given Betty a key and her telephone number is on the pad.'

I couldn't bear the thought of him being in the same building as that dreadful woman, never mind the idea of them still working closely together, but then I reminded myself quite forcefully that it was none of my business and, in any case, even if they never even spoke to each other again, the damage had already been done.

As if he had read my mind, Jack told me, 'It *is* over, you know.'

'But the damage has been done, hasn't it, Jack?' I said the words I'd been thinking out loud and very firmly. 'And, to be honest, I can't see any way forward for us now.'

'Not even for the baby?'

'Not even for the baby,' I repeated, 'because you and I both know that staying together for the sake of a child isn't a good enough reason.'

'Couldn't we even try?'

I had no idea why I hesitated over the answer even for a moment, because surely we both knew it would be pointless.

I shook my head and then, watching him leave, I wondered if I had just pushed Jack straight back into the arms of the other woman – and if it really mattered.

Chapter Seven

No sooner had Jack walked out of the front door, closing it with a little slam behind him, than it opened again and my mother walked in. Her sudden appearance made me jump. They'd obviously met on the drive and he'd opened the door for her, because she hadn't rung the doorbell and didn't possess a key.

'Do come in,' I said with a trace of sarcasm in my tone, which was obviously lost on my mother.

She followed me into the lounge and, taking in the nest of cushions and duvet awaiting me on the couch at a glance, she demanded, 'What's happened?'

'Didn't Jack...?' I began.

'He said you'd had a fall, when I phoned earlier, but not when, where or how – just that you were OK. So I came to find out for myself what happened. What about the b—'

'The baby is fine,' I cut in, 'but I'm covered in bruises and as stiff as you like, which is why I'm not going to work.'

'Do they know about...?'

'No, but Jack does. He's insisted on being here to take care of me and I'm not really in a position to argue.'

'But he's *not* here, is he?' she sounded indignant. 'Where

was he off to that's so important he would leave his pregnant wife – his injured pregnant wife – to her own devices?'

'He's had to go in to work,' I said shortly.

'To work?' My mother sounded scandalized. 'To work, and isn't that where he...?'

'Met that woman? Yes, she's his boss.'

'And you're happy to let him...?'

'I'm not his keeper, Mum. I'm his wife – for the moment.'

'Not that that stopped him.'

'Exactly,' I nodded, 'as I keep telling him – the damage has already been done.'

'Yes, but how can you two possibly work things out while he's still seeing that woman every day?'

I turned my back on her, rearranged the duvet to my satisfaction and took my time settling beneath it before I made any effort to deal with her question. Then I asked simply, 'May I ask who – exactly – mentioned the possibility of Jack and I "working things out"?'

'But ...' she hesitated, before continuing determinedly, 'I thought – you know – with the b—'

'You thought wrong,' I said flatly. 'After what's happened, it will take more than a baby to put things right between us.'

'So,' she sat down abruptly in the armchair opposite the couch I was lounging on, still wearing her coat, scarf and gloves and clutching her handbag, 'you're planning on being a single mother, are you?'

The thought was daunting – especially when it was said out loud like that, but I wasn't about to let my mother guess at any reservations I might have about lone parenthood.

'I didn't exactly plan any of this – it has all come as a complete surprise to me, as you very well know, Mum. I'm just trying to deal with what *is* in the only way I know how.'

I picked up the TV remote control as a strong hint that I had nothing further to say on the subject, and up popped Jeremy Kyle in full flow on the television. His style of programme seemed very apt under the circumstances and I wondered idly whether he could sort out the mess my life was in. From what I'd seen and heard of his programmes he did seem to have all the answers.

My mother ignored the hint, but her voice softened as she agreed, 'I know it has all come as a shock, and I know you are doing what you think best under the circumstances, Fay – I'm merely trying to advise you not to close your eyes to all of the various options open to you.' I just looked at her and then back to the argument kicking off on the television, but she continued anyway. 'I can understand that you're angry with Jack – and I admit you have every right to be—'

'That's big of you.'

'But—'

'She came here, you know,' I interrupted, not wanting to hear what else she had to say.

'Who?'

Again I just looked at my mother quizzically until the penny dropped, I could almost hear the clang when it did.

'You don't mean...? Not *her* – not *that* woman?'

'That's the one. I found her wandering around upstairs. She'd let herself in with Jack's key.' At my mother's outraged expression, I added with ill-concealed impatience, 'No, Mum, he obviously didn't give it to her, she took it from his pocket. She came here to tell me how much more she could offer him – but I kind of took the wind out of her sails by announcing that I was pregnant and wondering if she was able to offer him a child. That was when Jack walked in. To his credit he got rid of her pretty damn quick.'

Before we could say more, there was the sound of a key rattling in the Yale lock and someone entering. The next minute Betty popped her head around the lounge door.

'Oh good,' she said, 'you've got company.'

'Come and meet my Mum, Betty. Mum, this is Betty from next door. Jack asked her to keep an eye on me.'

'How nice to meet you,' Betty said, shaking my mother's hand briskly and offering in the same breath, 'I'll go and put the kettle on, shall I?' And she went off to do just that.

I'd never seen my mother look so put out. 'She seems very at home here. It appears she even has her own key – something I've never, ever been offered. I had no idea you were on such friendly terms with any of the neighbours,' she huffed, 'and Jack could and should have asked *me* to keep an eye on you – I am your mother, after all, Fay.'

'It's not a competition,' I sighed, 'Betty lives right next door *and* she used to be a midwife. You live across the other side of town and, to be honest, you seem a bit too keen, for my liking, for me to hurry up and bury the hatchet.' I paused as if I was giving the matter some thought, and then continued. 'Actually I might even have been tempted to do just that if I could bury it in Jack's head – rather than simply stick plasters over the gaping wound he has made in our marriage, which seems to be your only solution.'

'I'm only thinking about how much more difficult life will be for you as a single mother,' she protested. 'I know what Jack did is very, very wrong, but have you even talked to him about it?'

I leaned towards her and said in a very firm tone, 'I don't want to talk about things with Jack anymore. I've only let him back into the house because I'm nervous of something going wrong with the pregnancy after the fall.'

'Tea,' Betty announced brightly, bustling forward to set a tray on the coffee table. It was beautifully laid out with vaguely familiar cups and saucers that she must have found at the very back of a cupboard, because mugs were far more mine and Jack's style. She lifted a teapot I didn't ever recall using and poured a cup for each of us.

'This is nice, isn't it?' she asked brightly, and my mother and I agreed half-heartedly that it was.

'You haven't brought the dogs round with you,' I commented eventually, and frowned at my mother's appalled expression and the way she mouthed the word, '*Dogs?*' as if she was talking about some sort of vermin.

Thankfully Betty was pouring more tea, but she looked up, smiled and told us, 'No, I left them watching *This Morning* – they have a soft spot for Philip Schofield, you know. So they'll be absolutely fine until lunchtime.'

'Bless them.' I smiled back at her and thoroughly enjoyed my mother's bemused look.

'Now,' Betty leaned towards me, 'did you manage to have a soak in the bath – and has it helped at all?'

I could feel my face burning at the thought of the disastrous and highly embarrassing conclusion to my bath-time of the night before. I hoped it wasn't too obvious that I was actually blushing, but I was able to say, quite truthfully, that I thought it had helped a little.

'Just how serious was this fall?' my mother demanded. 'Only it's beginning to sound rather more than the simple trip in the street that Jack led me to believe it was.'

I was about to play it down, but Betty got in first to explain. 'It was a whole flight of concrete steps and that dreadful woman witnessed the whole thing, I believe.'

My mother looked aghast, as well she might. 'She didn't

have anything to do with you falling, did she?'

I shook my head. 'No, Mum, I don't think even she would stoop so far as to push me.'

'I wouldn't be so sure of that,' she began, 'I wouldn't put anything past someone who would steal her lover's key and then come snooping around his house ...'

It was Betty's turn to look appalled. 'She didn't.'

'She certainly did and what sort of person do you think does something like that?'

They were off then, any differences and petty jealousies on my mother's account forgotten as they agreed, in horrified tones that Iona sounded like a mad woman. I wasn't inclined to disagree.

'What Jack was thinking to get mixed up with someone like that, I don't know.' My mother shook her head.

'Well, he wasn't thinking, was he?' I said bluntly, adding a bit rudely, 'At least not with his head.'

They looked at me, and then at each other and then risked a little titter at my risqué remark.

'Men,' said my mother, and we all grimaced at each other.

'They're not all the same, are they, though?' I felt obliged to point out. 'Dad wasn't.'

My mother looked away and then seemed to think better of remaining silent, and turning back suddenly, she looked straight at me and said flatly, 'Oh, he had his moments.'

'Dad?' Sitting up straight, I stared at her, eyes wide with shock and absolutely scandalized. 'Not Dad?'

'He wasn't a saint, you know,' she said defensively.

'But Dad,' I repeated, aware of how stupid I sounded but unable to help myself.

'He begged me not to tell you, and I've kept my promise – until now. I just don't want you to think that Jack is the only decent man in the world to stray or that one mistake has to mean the end of what has otherwise been an extremely good marriage.'

'There are women out there with no scruples,' Betty put in, 'and men daft enough to fall for their wiles.'

'It works both ways, though, of course,' my mother put in, giving me another straight look. 'Have you never been tempted to stray, Fay? Because I know that I have.'

'*Mum*,' I said sharply and gawped at her. I couldn't believe it. She was an attractive woman, I knew that, but she'd never seemed even the tiniest bit interested in meeting anyone else in the five years since my father died, so why on earth would I have ever given a single thought to the fact she might have had a roving eye when he was still alive?

'Few of us are saints.' Even Betty seemed inclined to join in, and then she continued to my astonishment, 'There was this rather dishy doctor when I was doing my nurse training.' She smiled and stared dreamily across the room at a past memory we couldn't share.

'Did you?' my mother asked her nosily, and totally ignoring me shaking my head at her.

'Did I?' Betty met her look and then answered her cheeky question with what I could tell was the truth. 'Oh, I didn't do anything about it – but that doesn't mean I wasn't very tempted.'

'Me either,' said my mother, 'but I've always wondered what it would have been like.'

'*Mum*,' I gasped, feeling as if the world was turning upside down. For God's sake, it sounded as if my father had actually had a fling and my mother had seriously considered embarking on one of her own – and even Betty wasn't entirely guiltless. I could hardly believe it.

While I was still trying to gather my wits, they had changed the subject and were chatting away as if these shocking revelations had never been made. Left to my own devices, I felt obliged to spend time considering my mother's searching words, "Have you never been tempted, Fay?" and what my response might have been to her question – if she had waited for an answer.

Betty and my mother got up and left the room together, still chattering away as if they'd known each other all of their lives. Presumably they had told me where they were going and why, but my mind was far too full of my own thoughts to pay any heed. To the distant murmur of their voices and the homely sounds of them clattering around in the kitchen, I reluctantly allowed my mind to go back and to recall a time that I had tried very hard to forget. I had to admit I had completely succeeded. I hadn't given a thought to it in years. In fact, right up until my mother's words had forced me to remember.

It had all started so simply and easily, ridiculously so really, and all very innocent to start with. Jack was going away on a work-related matter only a relatively short time after the one last false alarm that had been instrumental in forcing us into accepting that our dream of becoming parents was never going to become a reality.

He had asked if I would be all right and I remember feeling that he should have known I still needed him to be with me, even while I was assuring him that I would be fine. Physically I *was* fine, but mentally I was still feeling fragile, not to mention a terrible failure. I knew Jack was anxious about leaving me, but I was still angry at him that he felt able to go anyway in spite of his reservations. I ignored his suggestion to ask my mother over to keep me company or to go and stay with her. I hoped thinking of me on my own at home would make him feel guilty.

It was Friday evening and I had worked on at the office long after everyone else had gone home for the weekend, just to pass the time. Knowing that Jack would already have left, I wasn't relishing the thought of the empty evening ahead at all.

The supermarket was all but deserted by the time I got there and it rankled that it appeared the majority of families and couples of Brankstone would already be cosily enjoying their home-cooked meals or their takeaways together. I didn't need reminding that I was quite capable of cooking myself a meal or ordering in a take-away, but I was too busy playing the martyr and too determined to make life difficult and even unpleasant for myself.

I detested ready meals, but there in my basket sat a lasagne for one, together with one of those individual bottles of wine, and a family sized jam roly-poly with custard which I intended to eat my way through even if it killed me. I was heading towards the confectionary aisle intent on purchasing the biggest bar of chocolate I could find – assuring myself that I *deserved* comfort food in copious amounts – when I clashed with possibly the only other shopper in the place so violently that our wire baskets locked together.

We looked at each other, and then at practically identical purchases and burst out laughing. After a futile attempt to separate our shopping we gave up and smiling, we took stock of each other.

He was as dark as Jack was fair, his eyes dark brown in contrast to the blue of Jack's. He was taller and leaner, and very easy on the eye, dressed as he was in black t-shirt and jeans. I could just tell that he liked what he saw, too, and was suddenly glad that I'd made an effort to dress up for work that morning in an attempt to make myself feel better. The floaty summer dress flattered my slim figure and I was still tanned from a recent holiday. We were both wearing wedding rings, I noticed.

'What would you say,' he began, with a cheeky grin, 'to us both ditching the junk food and keeping each other company over a proper meal – in a decent restaurant?'

'I would say yes,' I replied without hesitation and to my own surprise. I wasn't the kind of person who acted on impulse.

Without further discussion, we placed the entangled baskets and their contents on the supermarket floor and hurried, laughing riotously, as if we had done something very clever, from the store.

It wasn't actually the nicest restaurant I had ever been to, part of a chain of well-known pubs and eateries known for its value for money, but we quickly agreed that it would do because it was quite close by. We pulled up in our cars almost simultaneously, but he was there to open my door and I didn't miss the way he eyed my bare legs as I climbed from the car. I half-expected him to whistle, if I was being honest, but I guess that would have been a bit crass. I did quite like the fact he didn't try to hide the fact that he was attracted to me.

I felt a frisson of excitement at the thought of what I was doing as we walked across the car park, almost but not quite touching. Jack wouldn't have approved, that I was certain of, but a part of me thought it was his own fault for leaving me to my own devices when he was well aware I was still feeling vulnerable and a little unloved.

Anyway, I assured myself, it's just a meal. Just two people finding themselves alone for whatever reason and enjoying each other's company over a civilized meal – all perfectly open and above board. Even so, I instinctively knew I wouldn't be telling Jack about it.

I hadn't meant to drink, not with the car outside, but felt one glass of wine wouldn't hurt. He ordered a bottle of Pinot

Grigio without asking my preference – but that was fine. With the first glasses of wine, we relaxed into each other's company and once any awkwardness was dispelled, we talked easily about our likes and dislikes from stuff such as books and films to holiday destinations and all manner of other things.

What was never mentioned were the rings on our fingers, the reasons we were alone – obviously temporarily – on a Friday night or, indeed, anything personal at all. I'm pretty sure we didn't even exchange names. Without saying so we both knew this was a one off and that after this one evening, we would never see each other again.

It honestly started as nothing more than simple fun but, as we lingered over the meal and a second bottle of wine was ordered the atmosphere began to change, and what had started as friendly became distinctly flirty. We tasted food from each other's forks and when our fingers touched across the table it wasn't always by accident.

By the time we left the restaurant we could barely keep our hands off each other and when he kissed me, hard, pushing me back against my car door with his body, I made no demur. It was a long time since I'd felt like an object of anyone's desire and the fact that he wanted me was very obvious. Winding my arms around his neck I kissed him back with gusto.

'Is there anyone at home waiting for you?' He murmured the question, his breath tickling my ear, and the warmth of his tone and his close proximity sent the heat of my own desire racing through my veins. I felt more alive than I had in a very long time.

I wanted to turn away as he tilted my chin and looked into my eyes, but his gaze held mine steadily and I found that I couldn't look away – and that I really didn't want to.

'No,' I whispered.

I think he might have booked the room while he was settling the bill, because it was all too easy with the hotel right next door to the restaurant and we were clearly expected. To be honest, I was past caring by then and we were all over each other the minute the door closed behind us. It was as if any and all self-control had gone and sanity had finally flown out of the window – it was as if this moment was exactly what I had been waiting for.

Gathered close until it felt all the breath had been crushed out of me, I felt his body hard and demanding against mine, immediately eliciting an answering need in me. All sensible thought flew out of my head as we fell onto the bed together, scrabbling at each other's clothes, intent only on the pleasure that was sure to follow.

My phone suddenly burbling in my handbag just as he was about to enter me acted as a dash of very cold water on our over-heated senses and we both froze instantly.

The harsh sound of our breathing almost drowned out the cheerful little tune that played on and on insistently, bringing with it a hefty dollop of the common sense we had so carelessly thrown to the wind.

'Ignore it,' he said his voice still thick with the remnants of his desire, but he didn't sound very hopeful.

'I can't – and I can't do this anymore,' I said, putting my hands flat against his chest and pushing against him, belatedly aghast at my own sluttish behaviour. What on earth had I been thinking?

To his credit, he released me and rolled off immediately and, embarrassed now, we fumbled with buttons and zips until we looked respectable again. I gathered up my handbag with its now silent phone and left immediately without a backward glance.

I phoned for a taxi before I returned Jack's call. He was at home waiting for me, having had second thoughts and made his excuses to his colleagues. He accepted without hesitation my explanation about a drink with the girls from work that had turned into a few too many.

'You deserve to let your hair down after what you've been through,' he said, and I sobbed in the back of the cab all the way home at the thought of what I had almost done and what Jack would think of me if he ever found out.

Chapter Eight

I HUDDLED BENEATH THE duvet, sick to my soul all over again at what I had so very nearly done on that evening so long ago. At what I definitely *would* have done if Jack hadn't chosen that very moment to phone me on my mobile and broken the spell I was under. A one night stand, for God's sake, and me a happily married and supposedly mature woman. I'd never even contemplated such a thing when I was a flighty teenager.

The shameful memory of that night had been carefully buried for so many years that I had almost been able to convince myself that it had never happened at all – almost, but obviously not quite as was now apparent. How would I have ever explained to Jack the way I had allowed myself to be picked up by a complete stranger – in a supermarket of all places? Sharing a meal with a guy I'd only just met had been bad enough, and the memory made me cringe, but the certainty that I would have gone on to share my body with him made me feel the deepest disgust with myself all over again.

Who was I, really, to sit in judgement of Jack for what he had done – when I had so very nearly done the same thing myself? I felt my harsh attitude towards him begin to soften.

And then I sat up straighter and reminded myself, rather

forcefully, that *nearly* wasn't at all the same thing as actually doing the deed. OK, so it was only the ringing of my mobile that had brought me to my senses before anything actually happened – but at least my phone was turned on. Maybe if Jack hadn't been so meticulous in turning his mobile *off* when he was with his lover, he too might have been reminded that he had a wife at home. Not that he should have needed reminding, I thought, a tad piously.

The biggest difference between what I had *almost* done and what Jack *had* done, I reiterated, in an effort to make myself feel less guilty, was that my mistake would have been a very definite one off, while his affair had been ongoing, and I was convinced it would have continued indefinitely if he hadn't so clumsily given the game away on Christmas morning.

I felt better now that I had regained the moral high ground in my own mind, and swept my conscience clear. I even managed to do justice to the meal that my mother and Betty had prepared between them.

'It's only salad,' they had apologized rather more profusely than the tasty meal warranted as we took our places round the kitchen table, 'but there's nothing in it to cause you or the baby any harm.'

My mother then went on to reminisce at great length about all the things she had eaten and drunk while she was pregnant with me – and without any ill effects at all. It took Betty to point out that things were very different these days – what with all the additives and preservatives, not to mention all the new foods on offer – and that it was always better to be safe than sorry, especially given my history.

Her words made my mother clap a hand to her mouth, and then mutter that she hadn't been thinking and of course we had to be extremely careful and take no chances at all.

I didn't much like being reminded of the instability of my condition and the fact I'd never managed to carry a baby to full term so far.

'I'm halfway there, aren't I, Betty?' I turned to my neighbour. 'I've never reached this stage in a pregnancy before, so that's a good sign, isn't it?'

Betty nodded with great enthusiasm and hurried to reassure me. 'Oh, I would definitely say so. You've already suffered a great shock with this business of your husband's affair, not to mention the nasty fall, and all without suffering any apparent ill effects, which has to say something about the pregnancy. I think this baby is determined to survive and I'm quite sure your own midwife has been telling you the same thing. However, we still can't take anything for granted, not with your past experiences, so I would still recommend taking things very steadily and lots of rest will do you no harm at all.'

'My thoughts exactly.' We all turned at the sound of Jack's voice from the kitchen doorway. 'And that's why I think you should give your notice in at work as soon as possible.'

I stared at him and then demanded, 'Oh, really? Well, there might have been a time in our lives when such a thing was an option – but not now. Not given the changed circumstances we find ourselves in. How exactly do you suggest we manage for money with a baby to provide for, a divorce to pay for and new homes to buy and furnish? Not to mention buying expensive presents for the other woman in your life,' I added nastily.

My mother and Betty gasped out loud. Jack looked as if I had slapped him, and I was glad, even if I did realize that a lot of the self-loathing induced by memories much better forgotten had been redirected in his direction. He'd been the one having an affair – *not* me – I reminded myself. I stood up, threw a look of deep loathing in his direction and stalked from the room.

Jack found me huddled miserably into my duvet nest on the couch because, in truth, I had frightened myself with the graphic reminder of what lay ahead. It was all his fault, of course, and I scowled up at him.

His shoulders slumped, but he came and sat down in the chair opposite my spot on the couch. 'OK,' he said, and his face was sad, 'I accept that I've messed up big style, but there's no reason why you and the baby should suffer for my big fat mistake. Those things you mentioned in there,' he nodded towards the kitchen, 'surely they can wait. Do you really want to be dealing with the stress of a divorce, not to mention a house move in the middle of preparing for the birth of our first baby?'

I couldn't be bothered to point out – yet again – that it was entirely his fault I was even having to contemplate any of it, and just asked tiredly, 'So, what do you suggest?'

'Put the divorce and the house sale on hold for the time being. After all, what's the big rush?'

I could have said that there was my strong desire to be free of him. The end of a marriage signalled the end of a shared life as far as I was concerned, but common sense told me that, in our case it didn't – because there would always be the baby tying us firmly together. In the end I stayed silent, folded my arms across my chest and glared at him.

Undaunted he continued, 'I'm suggesting we stay put until the baby is safely born, stay married ditto. In the current economic climate, it takes forever to sell a house and you'll need a stable environment to bring the baby home to. Besides, what message are we giving the child in the future if we're divorced before he or she is even born?'

'Erm, that Daddy couldn't keep it in his trousers,' I suggested harshly, and enjoyed watching him squirm.

Ignoring my comment he said, 'I would like to stay on hand to take care of you through the remaining months of the pregnancy. I don't like the idea of you living here alone when anything might happen. I can also take on a bit of household maintenance ...'

I was laughing before Jack finished the sentence. 'You? I scoffed. 'Household maintenance? You've always got someone in to do any jobs that needed doing around here – however small. To my certain knowledge, you've never changed so much as a tap washer or painted a door frame in all of the years we've been married.'

'Then it's about time that I did,' he said firmly, refusing to be riled by the ridicule in my tone. 'As you've so rightly said, money is going to be tight and it will be cheaper if I stay put. We won't be the first couple to live separately under the same roof – or the last,' he added as an afterthought.

'Let me think about it,' I said, but I could tell that he already knew he had won – if only for now.

He was right that I couldn't let what was happening between us take my focus away from getting safely through this pregnancy. *Nothing* was more important than our baby. At my age, the fact that I had become pregnant at all had come as a huge surprise and the fact that I was still safely pregnant months on, given my history of miscarriage, the stress I'd been under, *and* the nasty fall, was nothing short of a blessed miracle. I knew that I could – and would – do whatever it took to ensure this baby was born safely, even if it meant living with my cheating husband for a while longer.

I accepted that the only real alternative to living with Jack was having my mother live with me and, much as I loved her, I couldn't face that. We got along fine in small doses, but being in each other's company twenty-four seven would surely be a recipe for complete disaster. She was far too fond of getting her own way – and so was I.

There was also – and I hated to admit it – the matter of 'what the neighbours would say', not to mention everyone at work. I knew I shouldn't mind, but I did – very much. No one likes to be made a fool of, and how would it look when it became known that my husband had been playing away from home, possibly for months, and I hadn't even noticed?

When we shared details of our future living arrangements, my mother was rather too delighted in my opinion. Oh yes, I could see the way her mind was working very clearly.

'This will be a *temporary* arrangement,' I said. 'We've just both agreed that the baby's health and safety must always come first. This is very probably our last chance to become parents – well, mine, anyway – and nothing, absolutely nothing, can be allowed to jeopardize that.'

'Well,' Betty said in her firm tone and with a brisk nod, 'I think you're both being very sensible. There's time enough to make plans for the future once the child is safely born.'

She was right – of course she was right – and her wise words made me begin to believe, probably for the first time, that one day very soon I *would* be a mother. I hadn't realized just how remote the possibility had become to me as I'd coped with one failed pregnancy after another.

Escaping back to work was going to be a huge relief because, once the bruising began to fade, the smothering began to get to me. Not from Betty, I had to say, because her belief that I would carry this baby to full-term rubbed off onto me and my confidence grew daily. After a few days with my feet up, she was encouraging me to go out and get some fresh air.

'Walking?' My mother sounded horrified. 'Do you think that's wise, Betty, given Fay's history of miscarriages, all the stress she's been under, and not to mention the fall? Surely a few more days ...'

'It's not just physical well-being that is important here,' Betty pointed out, 'there's her mental welfare as well. A gentle walk, not to mention a change of scenery will do Fay a world of good.'

'Well, you *were* a midwife, I suppose,' my mother said doubtfully.

'Yes, I was, Iris – and very good at my job I was, too. Now, slip your arms into this coat, Fay, and we'll be off. Just five minutes round the park and we'll be back for the nice cup of tea you'll have ready for us, Iris.'

'I can't thank you enough,' I told Betty as we set off up the road. My arm was safely tucked into the crook of Betty's and the dogs were at our heels. 'I was beginning to think I'd lost the use of my legs and was expecting my marbles to follow. How you managed to work it so that my mother stayed at home making tea, I'm not quite sure, but that's something else I can't thank you enough for. She'd be pushing me around in a wheelchair and treating me like an invalid if she had her way.'

Betty gave a sheepish little smile. 'I never dreamed I could be so bossy,' she said, 'but a positive attitude in any situation is far more helpful than forever looking on the black side, I've always found.'

We didn't hurry, stopping to pass the time with a couple of neighbours along the way. I even found myself sharing the news of my pregnancy – which I found reinforced the growing conviction that this time I really would eventually be holding a living and breathing child in my arms. The thought took my breath away and put a smile on my face.

My mother was on the doorstep when we arrived home, and she watched anxiously with her hands on her hips as we returned the three dogs to their home before making our way towards my own front door.

'Where on earth have you been?' She sounded frantic and had obviously worked herself up into a right state during our absence. 'You said five minutes, and that was at least fifteen minutes ago. What were you thinking, Betty, to be taking her on a route march all over town? I'd have thought you would know better, given Fay's hist—'

Ushering her quickly inside, I said furiously, 'Stop it, Mother – just stop it right now. I'm not a child and I'm not made of china. Do you *really* think I would do anything at all to endanger this pregnancy?' I glared at her. 'Well, do you? Go on, do you?"

'Well, no,' she admitted, 'but—'

'No buts, Mum. I'm a healthy pregnant woman. I am well aware of my history, but this time it's different from all those other times. I don't know why, I just know that it is. This baby is as determined to be born as I am to see it arrive into the world safely.'

She managed to stay silent, busying herself making the tea, but I could feel the disapproval emanating from her and understood that she would be far happier if she could keep me indefinitely on the couch, where she could keep a strict eye on me.

Luckily, both she and Jack gave up on the idea of trying to persuade me to give my notice at work in when they realized they were not only wasting their breath, but making me quite agitated into the bargain.

'Will you both stop treating me as if I'm an invalid or a

complete idiot?' I fumed. 'I'll be sitting at a desk, for heaven's sake, not working on a blasted building site. What harm can I possibly come to, tell me that? I promise to take the lift when I go to meetings and not climb flights of stairs, is there anything else you'd like to suggest?'

'Well, perhaps Jack could drive you to work,' my mother suggested, 'or they could reserve you a parking space near to the door?' And then she withered under my scathing look and finally gave up.

The first thing I did on the day I returned to work was to share the news of my pregnancy with the management and staff, and I was warmed by how thrilled everyone was for me. They were all aware of my unfortunate history of miscarriages but thankfully, no one mentioned it, but ooh-ed and ah-ed over the scan photos and asked when the baby was due. They seemed every bit as confident about this pregnancy as I was myself.

Fresh cups of tea appeared on my desk periodically, and no one made a trip to the canteen without asking me first if there was anything I would like brought back for elevenses or lunch.

It felt wonderful to immerse myself in work again and not to be thinking constantly about either the state of my health or my marriage. I felt no urge at all to share details of the latter with my colleagues.

'Jack must be *so* thrilled,' they said repeatedly, and I always replied that, of course, he was absolutely over the moon. That bit at least was the truth, and it was much easier to leave it at that than to spell out the reality of what he had been up to just prior to discovering he was about to become a father. I could imagine watching shock, horror and worst of all, pity, wipe the smiles from their faces – much easier to pretend for the few hours I spent at work each day that all was right with my home life.

True to his word, Jack got cracking with the paintbrush and roller whenever he got the chance, touching up paintwork that had become scuffed and discoloured over time. I couldn't say I was overjoyed that the whole house was reeking of paint, making me feel quite nauseous at times but, as January slipped into February and then into a very spring-like March, windows could be thrown open as the days grew warmer.

Jack was often home before me – though I refrained from querying the reason for the shorter hours – and various jobs around the house were undertaken with no prompting from me. Discovering a tap that had been dripping for months in the downstairs cloakroom had been treated to a brand new washer was the first indication that he was taking this property maintenance business seriously, and then there seemed to be no stopping him.

Loose doorknobs were tightened, a new showerhead fitted, and the filter replaced on the vacuum cleaner, among other things and, most surprising, a corkboard suddenly appeared on the kitchen wall with lots of advice on foods to avoid during pregnancy pinned to it.

My mother and Betty were frequent visitors, sometimes together and sometimes apart, and those were the times that Jack and I managed to put our differences aside for an hour or two and behave in a civilized manner. When we were on our own we had little to say to one another – and for that I had to take responsibility because I rebuffed any and every invitation to 'talk things through', dismissing the notion as 'completely pointless'.

We usually ate together, mostly in silence, before going our separate ways in the same house during the evenings, unless we had company. I read a lot or watched television, and was usually in the lounge or upstairs in what had become 'my' bedroom as opposed to 'ours'. Jack often worked in the dining room, spreading his paperwork across the table or he would shut himself away in his office. It worked after a fashion and, if I missed Jack's company I absolutely refused to admit any such thing.

I came home once to find him looking rather spruce in his best suit and a new shirt and tie. In spite of myself I did wonder what the occasion was. He didn't offer any indication about where he had been and I, of course, didn't ask. His life was his own – as was mine.

This being the case, I was surprised when he appeared behind me one evening just as I was lifting a casserole out of the oven, and said, 'That's that then, Fay, I've left my job.'

Chapter Nine

THE SHOCK OF Jack's bald statement almost made me drop the hot casserole dish and its steaming contents all over the floor. I recovered and carried it to the table, but it was all that I could do not to slam it down with force onto the heat proof mat and berate him furiously for his stupidity, and point out the dreadful accident he had almost caused.

Instead I took a deep breath, set it down carefully and, after closing my eyes and counting to ten, I turned slowly to face him.

'You've left your job, have you, Jack? What exactly is that supposed to mean?' I demanded. 'You've been sacked, you've been made redundant, or you've walked out? Which is it?'

If it was the first, I was already wondering whether we could claim for unfair dismissal. I was pretty sure you couldn't just sack someone because they refused to continue an affair, and neither could you dismiss someone because it was you who no longer wanted to be involved with them. I had no way of knowing which applied in this case because – though Jack had assured me at Christmas that the affair was over – backed into a corner, as he was, I felt he would say that.

If he'd been telling the truth, I also had no way of knowing whether or not it had started up again or indeed if it ever had finished. The temptation must have been strong simply to pick up where they'd left off since Jack and Iona had continued to work together every day, and Jack and I had been living a completely sexless existence since the festive bombshell was dropped, bringing an abrupt halt to any intimacy between us.

'None of those,' he said with a trace of smugness, bringing the dish of steamed vegetables to the table, and then pouring water from the filter jug into the waiting tumblers. 'I recently applied for another job and got it. I just finished working out my notice today. In fact, it's more of a transfer within the same company and a step up for me. I'll be working at head office, but that's only in the next town so it won't even make too much difference to my travel time.'

'Oh,' I muttered feebly, sitting down quickly in the chair he held out for me. 'Why haven't you said anything about this to me before?'

'We've hardly been what you would call chatty for some time, have we?' he pointed out – a fact that I couldn't deny, especially when he continued, 'If I'd have said, "can we talk?" you'd have said there was nothing to talk about. It's what you always say.'

This was so true that I concentrated on helping myself to vegetables and bit back the retort that, of the limited topics up for discussion in this house, the affair wasn't something I felt the least bit inclined to talk about or that he could hardly expect me to take an interest in his day to day working life when it involved that woman.

'I talk to you about the baby,' I said, feeling obliged to defend myself, without knowing why. What had I done wrong, after all? 'Let you know what the midwife has to say.'

'Yes,' Jack agreed, 'and I'm grateful to be involved. I know you don't think I deserve it.'

'Did I say that?' I kept my voice even and continued eating – though it was the last thing I wanted to do and every mouthful was all but choking me. It was a wonder I didn't suffer from permanent indigestion.

'Not in so many words, but I know it's what you're thinking, and I can hardly blame you. I messed up, Fay – yes, I know I messed up massively,' he added, correctly interpreting my look, 'but I would like to think that there is a way back for us – one day.' I noticed he was ignoring the food on his own plate to keep all of his attention on me.

'It's what keeps me going,' he added, 'that and the baby. I knew there would be absolutely no hope at all of us ever starting over again with Iona still in the picture frame – even if it was only in the capacity of boss. That's why I knew I had to get out of there.'

'Problem is,' I pulled a face, 'there are going to be available women wherever you work, Jack, and now that the trust has gone ...'

Jack's face suddenly darkened. 'So,' he almost snarled the word, 'you're prepared to throw away everything we ever had, rather than give me another chance.'

At his accusing words I pushed my plate forcefully away and stood up, with my hands flat on the table I leaned forward until we were face to face with only inches between us.

'How *dare* you,' I spat. 'How bloody dare you, you sanctimonious bastard. *You* threw away what we had, Jack. *You* – not *me*.'

He at least had the good grace to look abashed. 'OK,' he held up his hands, 'we're both in agreement about what I did and what that makes me, but am I *never* to be forgiven, Fay? Is there no way at all that we can talk through what happened and why?'

'What is talking about it supposed to achieve apart from making me angry all over again? I've never understood the so-called benefits, myself. Talking about it won't make the affair 'un-happen', but it will probably make me relive Christmas day all over again.'

'What about counselling? Would that help?'

I could tell by Jack's tone of voice that he was beginning to get desperate and that he, at least, was willing to try practically anything. The trouble was I was beginning to realize and accept that the only thing that was going to work for me was to be absolutely assured that the bloody affair had never happened in the first place. I just couldn't find my way past it – or get over it.

'That would just be more of the same. I would feel obliged to talk about something I don't want to talk about, but with yet another person involved – someone I don't even know.'

'And that bothers you?' Jack asked curiously.

'Yes.' I finally stood up straight, and then turned away from Jack as I searched for something that would describe the way I was feeling. 'Because – because I'm *embarrassed.*' Even as I said the word I knew it was the right one, the word I had been looking for.

'Embarrassed?' I felt rather than saw Jack come to stand behind me. 'But why? I'm clearly the one in the wrong.'

'Then why do I feel like such a failure?' I demanded, turning back to face him, astonished to find tears filling my eyes and pouring down my cheeks. 'Why do I feel as if, somehow, what has happened is all *my* fault?'

'Oh, Fay.' His voice broke and I was sure that if I looked there would be tears in his eyes, too. 'What have I done to you? To us? I'm so, so sorry.'

He stepped closer and then, a little hesitantly, he reached

out and put his arms around me and tried to draw me close. I stood stiff and unyielding, but couldn't quite bring myself to pull away entirely. Eventually I relented and slumped into his arms and, in spite of everything that had happened, for a brief moment it felt like going home.

'How could you do it, Jack?' I cried, suddenly coming to my senses, pushing him away and pummelling his chest in an absolute fury. It was such a relief to allow all the anger, the bitterness and disappointment that I had been keeping buried to be expressed. 'How *could* you?'

Somehow we found ourselves in the lounge. I huddled into the corner of the couch, shivering and, amazingly, realized I was far more upset than I had been when the affair had first come to light. I could only guess that the shock of it had been protecting me then. Jack found a throw and wrapped it around me, and then he sat down himself in the chair opposite.

'I don't know, Fay, I just don't know.'

'She's very attractive,' I found myself saying.

'But not even anything like my type.' Jack grimaced and shook his head. 'She's a go-getting, hard-faced career woman. I actually found her bloody scary to start with – and then ...'

'Then ...' I prompted, quite unable to believe that I was actually asking for details.

'Then I was kind of flattered when she started making it clear that she liked me – found me attractive – when it was quite clear to everyone that she could have any man that she wanted.'

'Probably saw you as a challenge,' I suggested, adding, 'not that you're unattractive. Of course you're not.'

'She was always there,' he went on. 'Sometimes I felt I couldn't move for her, couldn't get a coffee or a sandwich without her appearing beside me and then – stupidly, I suppose

– then I started to feel flattered that she seemed to genuinely like my company, to value my opinion and judgement but, honestly, Fay, I never for one minute at that point thought there was anything in it. She always knew that I was happily married and unavailable. There were photos of you, me – us – all over my office.'

As if that would make any difference to someone like that, I thought. She was definitely a predator – but that didn't excuse Jack's behaviour in any way, shape, or form.

'How did it start?' I asked, I kept my tone hard, knowing without a doubt that I wasn't going to like the answer, however Jack wrapped it up to make it more palatable.

'There had been a bit of light flirting between us – it was always just a bit of fun as far as I was concerned,' he said, and I felt as if he had stabbed me, because I knew he would have been playing right into her hands and he should have known it, too.

'She was sometimes a bit too touchy feely for my taste,' he continued, 'but when she brushed against me I always thought it was by accident and she seemed to be the same way with everyone, to be honest. Then – then we worked late one night – the whole team, of course, and rewarded ourselves with a nice meal because we had landed a big account. It wasn't even her idea.' He shook his head. 'No, I'm quite sure that it wasn't.'

Actually, I rather doubted that. The suggestion of rewarding themselves with a meal might not have come out of Iona's mouth, but it would definitely have been she who planted the seed.

'Everyone had a little too much to drink, including me, and at the end of the evening we were queuing for taxis – having left all our cars at work and walked to the restaurant. It was freezing cold, I remember, and she wasn't wearing a coat or even a cardigan. I loaned her my suit jacket. We only shared a taxi so that I could get my jacket back.'

Oh, that was a clever move on her part. I was becoming impressed in spite of myself, just knowing that she would have been the one to suggest it, though I still wondered that Jack could have been so gullible that he couldn't see through something so obvious. Perhaps he was in too deep by then because he was only a man after all.

'I didn't realize she'd dismissed the taxi until I was standing on her front doorstep, waiting for her to give me back my jacket, and I heard it pull away. I know I should have just left, walked away and phoned another cab but – I didn't – I went inside for a night-cap, and that's when it happened.' Jack's voice had become little more than a whisper. He leaned forward, his head in his hands, quite unable to look at me.

The thing was – though Jack couldn't possibly have known it – I had been there in a very similar position except that, in my case it *didn't* happen, but my face still burned when I recalled how close I had come – and if sex *had* happened that night, would we have started a full-blown affair? Who could say? I had no way of knowing.

'I'm so ashamed,' Jack was saying. 'I completely accept that I should never have let it happen again after that first time, but at the start it was exciting, different and dangerous. I never loved her – how could I when she wasn't you? Most of the time I barely liked the woman, but though it was only ever about the sex I felt like a fly caught in a spider's web, and every time I tried to finish it the strands seemed to tighten.'

It was only ever about the sex, not only stabbed this time, but I could feel the knife being twisted as he said the words. But why, I wanted to cry, why wasn't I enough for you?

'The thing that gets me,' I said, my voice steady and me back in control again, 'is that it would clearly still have been going on if you hadn't made that stupid mistake with the Christmas presents.'

'No,' Jack sounded horrified, 'I wanted out, Fay – I swear to you. Long before Christmas I was desperate to end it, but I was out of my depth. The necklace was supposed to be a farewell gift. An affair was not something I ever wanted, but I couldn't seem to disentangle myself. The fact that I was involved with my own boss made it even more complicated because I had to work with the bloody woman every day.'

'My heart bleeds,' I said sourly.

'Mine does,' Jack said, 'and it did every single day. I can totally actually understand why you can't forgive me, because I can never forgive myself for what I've done to you. You didn't deserve any of this, and the fact that you were pregnant – even though I didn't know it – just makes things a million times worse.' He stood up suddenly. 'You were right all along when you told me to leave – to get out of your life. I left on Christmas day when you told me to because I was so shocked at being found out, and I knew I didn't have a leg to stand on, but this time I'm going to leave without being told because I completely accept that I don't deserve to stay.'

He looked utterly defeated as he made his way to the door. I should have felt relieved to see the back of him, but actually I just felt very scared at the thought of facing the rest of my pregnancy and the baby's birth without Jack to support me. I didn't need a midwife to tell me that none of it was going to be plain sailing at my age.

'Don't go, Jack,' I said, 'don't you *dare* walk out of that door and leave me to cope alone. Whatever you've done, you are still this baby's father and we both deserve your support.

Once the baby is born we may have to think again but, for the time being, your place is here – with us.'

He stopped in the doorway with his back to me – and then he slowly turned to face me. He sounded so humble as he said, so quietly that I could scarcely hear him, 'Thank you.'

'You don't have to thank me – and don't read too much into it.' I gave him a straight look. 'This is all about me now and what's best for me and for our baby. You, me and our marriage don't really come into it.'

'Thank you, anyway.' With that Jack turned and left the room.

Did I feel better for hearing details of the affair? I gave the matter some thought and decided reluctantly that I could at least see how it had happened. Well, I should, of course, since the same thing had so very nearly happened to me. Did I feel like baring my soul about that long ago incident to Jack? No, not really. As far as I was concerned, whoever said confession was good for the soul was very probably lying and we should stick to the here and now.

I had no difficulty accepting that Iona had instigated the affair. My very brief time in her company had left me in no doubt that she was the type of woman who saw what she wanted and went for it. The fact that people might get hurt along the way would not have come into the equation or given her conscience even the slightest prick.

Her words that day in this very house came back to me. "He was already mine – *mine*." and I was sure she'd believed that. "He was ready to leave you." She probably believed that, too, but I wasn't so sure that I did. If Jack really had been ready to leave me, then why hadn't he gone straight to her when I threw him out on Christmas day? It wasn't the baby that brought him back because he had absolutely no idea about the pregnancy at that point. Iona was wrong, Jack was still mine – if I wanted him.

I could hear him clearing away the remains of the discarded meal in the kitchen and tried – and failed – to picture my husband fitting into the kind of world that I could imagine Iona would inhabit. The kind of world where money mattered – a lot – and appearance meant everything. There would be no slobbing around in PJs on a weekend, no pushing a trolley round Waitrose and burying sneaky treats under the healthy fruit and veg, or eating fish and chips out of the paper while watching a rented DVD.

Jack only wore a suit for work or when it was strictly necessary and couldn't wait to change into jeans and a t-shirt when he got home. He would be a square peg in a round hole at cocktail parties, being decidedly more at home enjoying a pint and a packet of crisps, propping up the bar at his favourite pub while discussing the latest win by his favourite football team.

All of that was the proof, if I needed it, that Iona didn't really know Jack at all. What on earth had made her think that she did I couldn't imagine. And then, as I forced myself to picture them together, I knew I had the answer.

I had already worked out that appearance meant everything to someone like Iona. Indeed, to all intents and purposes she and Jack would appear to be the perfect couple. Any slight flaws she might have detected in his personality and habits she would ruthlessly have ironed out as she worked to turn him into what she wanted. Thinking about the life that had waited for him, I almost had it in my heart to feel sorry for Jack – almost, but not quite.

I took myself off up to bed before Jack had finished in the kitchen and I heard him come up to his study along the landing soon after. What he was finding to do in there was beyond me, since he had just left one job and had yet to start the new one. Packing up boxes by the sound of the bumps and scuffles that came to my ears – perhaps clearing out the old in order to make way for the new.

I was tired, probably due to the emotions that hearing Jack talk about his affair had stirred up in me, and yet I couldn't seem to drop off to sleep. I kept seeing Iona standing in front of me, her eyes glittering with dislike as she taunted me with the words, "I have nothing to fear from the likes of you."

How it must rankle her to have to accept that she had been wrong about that and had actually lost out to the woman she was so certain she had nothing to fear from. The thought actually gave me no pleasure, in fact, I felt the first flicker of unease.

Iona didn't strike me as the sort of woman who, once she had made her mind up that she wanted something – or somebody – would give up that easily and, for the first time I wondered at my own complacency in believing that she had.

Chapter Ten

IN THE COLD light of another day it was easy to convince myself that my fears regarding Iona were groundless. Men like Jack were probably ten a penny in her self-centred world. Like buses there would be another three along presently for her to choose from – I only hoped that next time she would pick someone who was actually free and willing to get involved with her. And then I wondered if the challenge of stealing someone else's man wouldn't be half of the enjoyment for a woman like that.

Life settled down and any lingering fears over my pregnancy were lulled as we headed into my thirtieth week of gestation. I had never reached anywhere near this stage in a pregnancy before and relished every kick and even the ungainly waddle I was developing. Even heartburn was a novelty to be enjoyed in an odd sort of way, and I was absolutely thrilled when I could finally justify treating myself to a pair of maternity trousers.

All sorts of little gifts for the baby started to appear on my desk at work and my mother actually took up knitting again when she saw the shawl Betty had crocheted. I was amazed at the pretty matinee jacket she proudly produced. Each item was carefully packed away into the drawer I had cleared in my bedroom for the purpose. I hadn't felt any urge to go on a spending spree myself because I was still a little afraid that any such action would be tempting fate. However, I was becoming cautiously optimistic as the weeks passed and the regular visits from my encouraging midwife, who was often accompanied by a student eager to learn, definitely helped.

'Look, you're doing everything you can for you and for the baby,' I was assured, 'resting when you can, but exercising with gentle walks, too, eating healthily ...'

'But what if he or she still comes early? I've miscarried before – more than once,' I fretted, hating myself for sounding so negative but still feeling it had to be said.

'So I see from your notes.' She patted my hand. 'But even at the stage you are now the baby stands a very good chance of survival. Worrying really won't help at all, you know. Have you discussed your concerns with your partner? Sometimes just talking about it helps.'

'Mmm,' I muttered non-committally, unable to explain to someone who was little more than a stranger that I wasn't in the habit of talking to my partner about anything much of importance anymore.

On the surface we were getting along famously, sharing the cooking, the housework and the shopping, just as we always had but, hanging over us all the time, were the difficult decisions we were going to have to make once the baby had arrived.

Sometimes my head felt as if it was going to explode as I veered towards giving Jack another chance, before almost immediately deciding that, since a leopard never changed its spots, what would be the point? How was I going to feel if I opened my heart and let him back in, only for him to do exactly the same thing over again? How much worse would that be when there was a child at the heart of our family?

Life went on much as before, but always with the cloud of Jack's past conduct and the future consequences always hanging over me. So, when the first complaint about me was received at the university, I wasn't even that surprised given that my mind was clearly on other things. However, I was taken aback that it apparently came from a potential student and a mature one at that, complaining about my abrupt and unhelpful manner. I prided myself that my telephone manner was never less than exemplary and I always went out of my way to help and offer advice and guidance to visitors on Open Days.

My superior was as startled as I was. Peter Lucas shook his head, looked baffled and said he had trouble believing that I had ever been rude to anyone in my entire life.

'It's just not in your nature but, of course, all complaints have to be followed up and this one named you specifically. However, you know you have my full support and I will be making it clear that I don't doubt your integrity, not even for a minute.'

When a second complaint from another source followed the first, it began to look more serious, until letters to both of the senders were returned 'address unknown,' and then it was decided to drop the matter, though it still left a nasty taste in my mouth that someone out there obviously had it in for me. Such a thing had never happened to me before, not ever in all my years of employment at the university.

However, it was all forgotten when, at the end of March I safely reached the thirty-second week of my pregnancy. Even I could accept that at this stage, should I go into early labour, my baby would have an excellent chance of survival, and I finally allowed myself a quick visit to Mothercare on my way home from work as a sort of celebration.

I promised myself I wouldn't go mad and definitely wouldn't buy any big items, perhaps just some vests and baby-gros, because you couldn't have too many of those. Once through the door though, I found it desperately hard to stick to my promise and I soon became completely enthralled with the little hats, tiny socks, not to mention the miniature dunga-rees and the prettiest dresses. I spent ages fingering frills and flounces before giving in to the urge and putting several of those items into a basket that was already bulging with wipes, powder, lotion and all manner of other baby toiletries.

I was on my way to the till when I was halted by an elderly lady who hesitantly put her hand on my arm. 'Excuse me, my dear,' she began, and then stopped as if she didn't quite know how to continue.

The basket was heavy and the handles were cutting into my fingers, added to that when my shoulder bag wasn't digging into the flesh at the top of my am, it kept slipping down. I was also in a hurry to get home by this time, but the worried look on her face and the concern in her eyes made me stay.

'Is there something I can help you with?' I asked, hiding my impatience while wondering if she wanted some help with a purchase and, if so, why she hadn't asked the sales assistant standing nearby, doing nothing much more than twiddling her fingers.

'Well,' she began, and then rushed on as if she had suddenly found the courage from somewhere to continue with what-ever it was she needed to say, 'it's just that I'm almost sure I saw that lady slip something into your bag.' She turned and I turned with her, my gaze following the shaky finger she was pointing, and then she said, 'Oh, she's gone. Now you'll think I'm quite mad, but really, she caught my eye because she was standing so close to you, and I'm almost sure … But perhaps I was mistaken.'

'There's only one way to find out, isn't there?' I said, smiling down into the wrinkled face with its troubled expression. Apart from the concerned look in her eyes she appeared to be the picture perfect pensioner out to buy a little present for the latest addition to the family, and I had no doubt in my mind that her intrusion was well intentioned.

I placed the basket full of goods on the floor, unmindful of the contents spilling out, and pulled my over-sized handbag down from the crook of my arm. The zipped top was open – I'd always been careless about such things because the sleepy town of Brankstone was hardly the crowded city of London which we were led to believe was teeming with pickpockets.

Taking both handles I wrenched the bag wide open and looked for my purse first. There it was, along with my mobile phone, diary, spare tights, tissues, lipsticks and all the rest of the clutter I deemed necessary for day to day living – and then I saw an unfamiliar package nestling there.

The elderly lady pounced. 'There it is,' she said triumphantly, waving it under my nose. 'I didn't think I was wrong, but why would anybody…?'

The boxed item was a baby monitor, small but expensive at £99.99.

'That's exactly what I was asking myself,' I confessed, but with only the briefest moment of thought I was pretty sure I had the answer to that question, and immediately felt sick – sick and angry. 'You couldn't describe this lady to me, could you?'

'Oh, yes,' the grey-haired lady said, and nodded emphatically, 'because she was really quite lovely. She had long black hair, was tall and slim and beautifully dressed. Do you know her then?'

'I think so. It was probably her idea of a joke.'

'But she could have got you into a lot of trouble.'

I nodded again and keeping my voice steady, I said, 'I do realize that, but thanks to you it won't happen now.'

I found I was shaking as I added the package to the basket of my intended purchases. Not that I wanted it, but I felt I needed some kind of proof of what had just happened.

At the till, I paid for my own purchases and asked the assistant to include the old lady's items to my total – I felt it was the least I could do. Walking from the shop I could only imagine how shocked I would have felt with the alarm suddenly going off, the hand on my shoulder, and the shock of the unpaid item being found in my bag. It made me feel increasingly ill.

'My dear, you've gone very pale, perhaps we should find you somewhere to sit down.'

'No, I'll be fine,' I assured her, forcing a smile on my face. 'My car is close by and I'll be home in no time at all. In fact, can I offer you a lift? It really is the least I can do.'

'Bless you, no. I live close by – just above the convenience store there – but thank you, anyway. You should tell that friend of yours that what she did was extremely foolish. It wasn't at all funny and it might have got you into very serious bother.'

I didn't tell her that I thought that was the intention, just thanked her again and waved goodbye. I looked around the street as I walked the short distance to my car but there was no sign of the beautiful lady with the black hair – I hadn't expected that there would be.

My mother and Betty had already let themselves in and were busy in the kitchen preparing a meal when I arrived. They came regularly on pre-arranged visits as my pregnancy advanced, determined to make sure I put my feet up at the end of a working day. The television was on and through the open door I could see two of Betty's dogs sitting in front of the screen, their attention was glued to *Deal Or No Deal*. Only Gemma was willing to tear herself away from Noel Edmunds to come and greet me at the door. I noticed that my hand was still shaking when I reached out to smooth her head.

'You're late,' my mother put her head round the kitchen door, and then, looking pleased, she said, 'Oh, you've been shopping for baby things,' as she watched me drop the bulging carrier bags emblazoned with the store's name onto the hall floor.

When I didn't reply, but just stood there with Gemma beside me, she hurried towards me and her tone was sharp as she queried, 'What is it? What's happened, Fay? You look as if someone's just walked over your grave.' Taking my hand, she led me towards the kitchen, exclaiming as she did so, 'Your hands are like ice. Betty, get the kettle on quickly.'

It wasn't until I was sitting in the warmth of the kitchen with my hands wrapped around a cup of hot, sweet tea, and my mother and Betty standing over me, both staring down anxiously, that I was finally able to find the words to explain what had happened.

'But who would do such a thing?' I could tell that my mother was very shocked and, though she obviously didn't doubt what I was saying, she was finding it difficult to comprehend that anyone really would do such a thing.

'And why?' Betty added.

I didn't answer right away, just sipped my tea and stroked Gemma's head. It took a moment but when I looked up I could see understanding beginning to dawn in the two pairs of eyes.

'She wouldn't.'

'Surely not?'

'Can you think of anyone else who might have it in for me – because I can't. And,' I went on, 'now I think about it there have been other things, like Iona turning up here in this house and trying to intimidate me and, more recently, the letters of complaint about me that were sent to work.'

'You didn't say anything about complaints at work.' My mother was worried.

'Well, now that this has happened today I'm linking things together. The complaints could possibly have been genuine – there were two – but that's doubtful because when they were followed up – as complaints always are – the contact details on both letters turned out to be false and the names were nowhere on the system either.'

'And there were the flowers ...' Betty said, her voice trailing off as we turned to stare at her.

'What flowers?' Mum and I asked in unison.

'It was last month,' she explained, 'February. Yes, now I come to think about it – it would actually have been St Valentine's day.'

'*What* flowers?' we demanded, a little more forcefully.

'The dead ones,' she explained and, obviously thinking back, she added, 'all wrapped up in cellophane with a big bow tied round the stems. They must have been quite beautiful originally – you know with the roses and everything – but they were all quite dead.'

'Where were they, Betty?' I asked quietly, but I had already guessed the answer.

'They were left on your front doorstep, Fay. I put them straight in the bin, blaming mischievous children, but now I'm not so sure.'

My mother gasped out loud and started to ask again, 'But who would do...?' And then she stopped, before muttering,

'Her – that woman – she would actually do all of those things? But why?'

The front door slammed at that point and we all visibly jumped even though we were well aware it would just be Jack arriving home. I felt a huge surge of antagonism towards him for bringing this dreadful, vindictive, and obviously unstable woman into my life, and when Gemma went to meet him, wagging her tail, it seemed like another betrayal.

He came into the kitchen and, obviously having spotted the bags, he was beaming all over his face and said chirpily, 'You've been shopping, Fay.'

His tone was all pleased and light-hearted and, desperate to burst his happy bubble, I erupted furiously, 'Yes, and almost got arrested for shoplifting for my pains – thanks to *you*.'

I was on my feet by that time and he stepped back, away from the rage emanating from me and held his hands up as if to fend me off. 'Sorry,' he said, 'but you've lost me. Shoplifting? My fault?'

All three of us were talking and shouting at him at once, but somehow Jack got the gist of it and the colour drained from his face.

'She wouldn't …' he began, but the expression on his face told us clearly that he believed otherwise, even before we all yelled, '*Yes*, she *would*.'

As we began to list the other incidents previously dismissed, various happenings came to the mind of each of us.

'There was that nail in your tyre,' my mother recalled, 'and the scratch along your car door.'

'The time your bin was tipped over, scattering rubbish everywhere,' Betty reminded me.

'I'm going to phone the police,' Jack said, taking his mobile from his pocket and starting to programme in the numbers.

'And tell them what?' I asked, reaching out to take the phone from his hand. 'None of this is conclusive, is it? I could have driven over the nail – the wind could have blown the bin over ...'

'But it wasn't windy that day,' Betty protested, 'and no one else's bin fell over – just yours.'

'It's all just nuisance stuff,' I pointed out, 'nothing that can be taken seriously. Even the complaints could have been made by anyone, and regarding the shop-lifting incident, we only actually have a very elderly lady's eye witness account of what might have happened. I could have knocked the baby monitor into my bag in passing – I *was* loaded down with purchases at the time.' I put my hand up to silence the protests. 'I know that's not what any of us thinks happened, but we have no real proof, whatever we *suspect*.'

'I'll go and have a word with her,' Jack said, 'ask her what the hell she's playing at.'

'*No.*' My tone was emphatic. 'You'll do no such thing, Jack. We'll just ignore it and hope she loses interest. She's doing it for attention – she's that sort of woman – and if you go marching round there you'll be playing right into her hands. She would deny the whole thing anyway and probably try to convince you that your wife is paranoid.'

'You can't just let her get away with it.' My mother was outraged. 'She's obviously unhinged and must be stopped.'

'The only thing that will make her stop is to give her what she wants ...' I paused and they all stared at me, and then they gasped as I added, 'Jack.'

Chapter Eleven

'YOU CAN'T BE serious, surely?' Betty was the first one to speak and she sounded horrified. 'Are you telling us that you honestly believe that woman is making a nuisance of herself because she thinks that sort of behaviour will get Jack to continue the affair with her?'

'I think she's letting me know that she *is* serious and isn't about to give up. What do *you* think, Jack? You obviously know her better than anyone.' I added the last sarcastically.

'I think you might be right, on reflection. She is one very determined lady – there's no doubt about that – it's how I ended up entangled with her in the first place. And yes, I do know I behaved like a complete bloody idiot.' He had clearly correctly interpreted the look on my face.

Then he looked thoughtful and continued, 'Now I think about it, there were rumours about why she was transferred from her previous branch of the firm – after all, for someone like Iona, a backwater like Brankstone can hardly compete with the attractions of the city of London – though there was never anything definite. It was all very soon forgotten – probably because she was obviously extremely good at her job. Also,' he looked suddenly thoughtful, 'when I requested a transfer, no one seemed surprised and then it was all arranged very quickly.'

'I hope you realize, Jack,' my mother joined in to say scathingly, 'that your thoughtless behaviour, your utter stupidity, might have put your wife and baby – if not in danger – at least under some sort of threat. After all, what will this woman do next?'

'You can't think any less of me than I think of myself, Iris,' Jack assured her, raking a shaking hand through his fair hair. He turned to me. 'I can apologize until I'm blue in the face, Fay, but I'm aware it won't change anything. What do you suggest I – we – do?'

'For the moment – nothing.' I shrugged, because I really did feel at a loss. 'After all, what can we do apart from log details of every incident that we think has happened so far, and be on our guard?'

'You must never be alone in the house, Fay,' my mother said seriously, 'or even anywhere else for that matter. No more going shopping unless one of us is with you.'

It was very telling that no one disagreed with her and a rota was quickly worked out so that someone would be with me from the time I got home from work each day. If my mother or Jack weren't available, I would go to Betty's or she would be waiting indoors for me. We all agreed there was too much at stake to take any chances.

After a very short time it did begin to feel rather over the top to be making sure I left the house each morning at the same time as Jack, and to be phoning ahead at the end of each working day to make sure someone was at home waiting for me – especially because there was no further sign of Iona or any pranks that might be attributed to her. I decided that she had probably already set her sights on someone else's husband, or she might even have decided to get a life that didn't include Jack.

'I think she's definitely got the message,' I said, feeling a growing confidence as March slipped into April and my pregnancy continued safely.

However, between us we had made a comprehensive list of every single incident that could possibly have been connected with Iona, even finding ourselves adding unlikely things like cold calls when no one actually spoke on the telephone, quite obvious scam emails on the computer and charity bags pushed through the door.

It was true there had been nothing lately, but as my mother so rightly and so firmly said, 'You can't be too careful,' and reluctantly I felt obliged to agree, though I was beginning to feel stifled and noticed a desperate growing need for my own space.

I think Jack was aware of this, because when neither Betty nor my mother was in the house he appeared to be making a conscious effort to stay out of my way and we could usually be found in separate rooms in the house. He seemed to be settling into his new place of work, though he said very little about it, and paperwork was once more scattered over the dining room table. I confess I found that a bit odd when he had a perfectly good office upstairs, especially as he spent a fair bit of time there as well. Perhaps working downstairs some of the time was his way of keeping an eye on me.

He had finished touching up paintwork around the house, but was still keeping on top of household repairs, I was pleased to note, and seemed to be coming quite adept with hammer and screwdriver. I only had to mention a repair and it was done. At one point he even started making noises about adding what he called 'feature walls' to some of the rooms using contrasting wallpaper, and a pasting table had appeared from somewhere for a while. When it quietly disappeared again shortly afterwards, I simply assumed he had changed his mind. As I didn't think such a thing would make a scrap of difference when it came to selling the house, I didn't bother to mention it, and made the suggestion instead that he make a start on tidying the garden now that the days were getting warmer and the evenings lighter.

'It'll save money if you mow the grass yourself, rather than paying someone else to do it,' I pointed out as we stood side by side in the back garden, making a rough inventory of what needed doing.

'We don't have a mower,' Jack was quick to remind me.

'I do.' Betty's voice came through the shrubs that separated our properties and then her smiling face popped up over the top when she found something to stand on. 'You'd be welcome to use that, Jack. It's an electric one with a box on the front so you won't need to push too hard or rake up grass. It was working when I put it away after I last used it, but I suppose it might need a bit of oiling or something before it's ready for use.'

'There you are.' I found myself smirking. 'If Betty can manage to mow her own grass I don't think there's any excuse you can offer not to sort ours out. What with mowing and digging borders, you'll be fit in no time and without paying gym membership. We'll be quids in all round. As an accountant you must know it makes sense.'

'I'll come round right now and collect it, Betty, and as repayment for the loan of the mower, I'll take care of your garden, too.'

'You can't say no to an offer like that,' I told her with another smirk, 'or to the offer of a cup of tea. I was just about to put the kettle on, so come on round when you're ready and be sure to bring the dogs with you.'

'This is how it was years ago,' Jack said as he came clanking through the side gate with the mower, closely followed by Betty and Gemma. 'When I was growing up, my dad always did the gardening on Saturday and washed the car on Sunday. The whole street did the same.'

'Now there's another thought.' I nodded approvingly. 'Think how much we'd save on the valeting of two cars *and* the gardener's fees, and I'm sure you'd do a much better job of both.' I turned to Betty then to ask, 'Just Gemma again, is it, Betty? Not something I said to Zoe and Sadie, I hope?'

She shook her head and laughed. 'I'm afraid you just can't compete with a classic episode of *All Creatures Great And Small*, Fay. They just love that actor who plays James Herriot.'

'Well, it's always lovely to see you, Gemma, and I appreciate the sacrifice you've made, because I like Christopher Timothy, too,' I said warmly, as she followed me into the house and waited patiently for the biscuit she knew would be coming her way.

'More of a community feel to neighbourhoods in those days, wasn't there, Betty?' Jack was saying as he parked the mower outside the back door and came inside.

'Oh, yes. We all looked out for each other years ago. Everyone is so busy these days and even mothers of quite young children have to work to help pay the mortgage. Will you be going back to work?' she asked suddenly, catching me by surprise.

'Yes,' I said.

'No,' Jack said.

'The truth is that I suppose we haven't given any real thought to what happens after the birth,' I confessed, 'mainly because we've never got this far with a pregnancy before. I still have trouble believing it.' I cupped my hands protectively over the growing swell of my belly and was reassured to feel the baby kick strongly against my fingers.

And the truth is, I found myself confessing, but only to myself, that I'm so terrified of jinxing anything that I won't *let* myself think that far ahead or attempt to make any decisions. One day at a time, with what was to me still a miracle pregnancy, and one day at a time with Jack and our damaged marriage was all I could deal with. Here and now is all we really have and that was quite enough for me to be getting on with.

'Well, it won't be long now,' Betty smiled understandingly. 'I know Iris is getting very excited. What about your parents, Jack?'

'Both long dead, I'm afraid. That's the problem with being an older parent yourself, and mine weren't youngsters when they had me. I think I was a bit of an after-thought, to be honest, and my siblings are all a lot older and live in various countries overseas.'

'Australia, New Zealand and America.' I ticked the countries off on my fingertips. 'There's very little contact between us and I have no brothers or sisters. Poor baby.' I rubbed my belly again. 'It will have just the one grandmother.' I paused and then had a marvellous thought and went on, 'Unless you'd like to be an honorary one, Betty?'

Her face was a picture of complete and utter joy. 'Do you mean it, both of you?' she said, and Jack jumped in to say we would both be absolutely delighted. 'Oh, Gemma.' She took the dog's sweet face between her two hands, 'You're going to be an auntie.'

'Apart from my Mum we're a bit thin on the ground with friends, too,' I started to explain, 'we've not been that sociable in later years. All the couples we used to be friends with had families long ago and, with every failed pregnancy for us and every new birth for them, we found it more and more difficult to be in their company. Not that we grudged them their families, far from it, but they just seemed to pop out babies so easily and being around them made our problems and sadness that much harder to bear.'

'That's understandable,' Betty agreed, 'but I'm sure you'll make new friends once the little one is here. Babies are great ice-breakers.'

'Was that part of the problem?' I asked Jack after Betty had left, with Gemma trailing reluctantly and pausing to look back at me, obviously hoping for one more biscuit.

'Was what part of what problem?' he asked, hesitating at the back door, probably on his way to give the newly acquired mower a once over, followed by a test drive.

'Lack of a social life, lack of friends, we'd become quite insular over the last few years, hadn't we?' It was the first time I'd thought about it. 'You must have missed ...'

Jack came back into the room and straight across to me. He reached out, as if to take me by my shoulders, but then he thought better of it. We'd barely touched each other at all since Christmas day. I knew that was down to me but had felt no real desire to change things.

He stood in front of me, looked right into my eyes and said firmly, 'I haven't missed anything, Fay. Despite how it might look to you now, you were always enough for me. I wasn't looking ... I didn't want... It just happened, and I will spend the rest of my life regretting that it did.'

'And so will I,' I said, 'so will I.'

I watched through the window as he carried the mower up the garden. It was only a short time later that I heard the machine start up and the soothing hum as it went backwards and forwards across the lawn.

'It's not that neat,' Jack explained when I called him in for a lunchtime sandwich, 'with it being the first cut and all, Betty advised me to set the blades high – but next time …'

I wasn't really listening. The day was warming up nicely outside and Jack had removed his top. I found myself staring at him across the table. With all that had gone on I had all but forgotten how attractive I'd always found him. My mouth had gone quite dry and I found my fingers itched to reach out and touch the familiar firm flesh. For the first time in months, I could feel the heat of desire flickering through my veins.

I suddenly noticed Jack had stopped speaking and was staring at me. 'What is it, Fay? What's the matter? Is it the baby?'

'The baby?' I managed a laugh and it sounded shrill and a bit silly to my own ears. 'Oh, yes, the baby – I think it's going to be a footballer whether it's a girl or a boy – and that was definitely a goal.' I rubbed my bump as if there had been an extra hard kick.

'Can I feel?' It was the first time Jack had asked. The first time he had probably even dared to ask for fear he would get his head bitten off. I found I had it in me to feel a little bit sorry for him – even while I was telling myself he had brought this whole sorry situation onto himself.

'Yes, of course,' I said, keeping my tone as natural as I could.

He was round to my side of the table in seconds, and dropping to his knees beside my chair, he reached out a tentative hand. He hovered over the swell of my belly and looked at me. I took his hand and placed it where the baby was most likely to kick.

Aware that I had invented a foetal movement that hadn't actually happened, I let go of his hand and muttered under my breath, 'Come on, baby, show Daddy what you can do.'

I think we were both holding our breath, and we stayed like that in a silent tableau that seemed to last forever. Jack's hand was warm through the smock I was wearing. I stared down at the familiar crinkle of the hair at his nape, noting that he needed a haircut, smelling the familiar aroma of his cologne and the male scent of his body – and, I knew, the strongest sense of longing that we could only go back to the way we were before.

And then right on cue, the baby – our baby – moved, and when Jack looked up at me there was complete wonder in his eyes. The next moment we were both crying as if our hearts would break and I had gathered him into my arms, but the moment after that we were kissing.

I knew Jack wanted me – I wanted him, too – but I was the first one to come to my senses.

'We can't, we mustn't ...' I pushed him away, and we both knew that it wasn't just the baby I was thinking of. 'I can't,' I said firmly. 'To be truthful, I don't know if I ever can again.'

'And I don't have it in me to blame you,' Jack said, 'but thank you anyway for giving me a moment when, for a while, I could actually believe that anything might be possible. I'll try to keep believing that it might be at some time in the future.' He turned away, and then turned back and smiled, 'Feeling our baby move is totally amazing.'

'Yes, it is,' I said softly.

Jack went back to his mowing, and I pottered around the house, tidying, dusting and collecting laundry, which I carried downstairs to the utility room and loaded into the washing machine. I couldn't hear the mower, so thought it likely that

Jack had finished our lawn and gone next door to make a start on Betty's.

I was folding towels and looking out of the window when I noticed a movement in the shed at the bottom of the garden. At first I thought it was Jack, and thought no more of it but, as I glanced again, the person came close to the window. I could see that whoever it was quite obviously had dark hair and not fair, and it was long instead of short. I immediately froze on the spot.

It was her. Who else could it be? She must have been hiding there, waiting for Jack to leave. I dropped the towels in a panic as the shed door opened and turning quickly, I bumped into the ironing board which went crashing to the floor, taking the iron with it. Stumbling in my haste, I banged my shin against the stool I sat on to do the ironing and on legs that had turned to rubber, I made my way into the kitchen and rushed towards the open door.

I slammed it shut so hard that I was surprised the glass panes remained intact, and the key rattled as I struggled to turn it in the lock. Just to be on the safe side I shot the bolt across and looked up just in time to see a male stranger with long black hair making his way back down the garden carrying a rake. He looked at me curiously before making his way round the side of the house.

Chapter Twelve

'IT WAS A neighbour, Fay, just a neighbour.'

Jack had come in to find me a trembling wreck; weak tears streamed down my face, and I was so cold to his touch that he had immediately turned the heating right up, wrapped me tightly in a warm throw and placed a cup of hot tea in my hands.

'Surely you didn't think ...' he stared at me. 'You did, didn't you? You thought it was *her*.'

I nodded and shivered so much that my teeth actually chattered. 'All I could see was a person in the shed and the black hair,' I sobbed, 'and you were nowhere to be seen.'

'Oh God,' he groaned, 'I'm so sorry. I just didn't think.'

'Evidently,' I said, finally managing to get a grip on my shattered nerves and feeling absolute fury take the place of fear, 'and that's exactly how we got into this mess in the first place, isn't it? I don't know how much longer I can live like this, Jack.'

I knew I was being paranoid about the bloody woman but I couldn't seem to help it. If I was being sensible I might be able to accept that, since her childish attempts to cause trouble for me at work had obviously failed, and then the effort to incriminate me in Mothercare had been aborted, she had probably lost interest in her persecution of me. However, I had no way of knowing that for sure and, as long as she continued to feel like a threat, there was definitely not a hope in hell of a future for Jack and me.

Jack cooked the meal and cleared up afterwards. He made sure I was settled on the couch with everything I needed, sorted out my favourite DVD, and then asked me if I would prefer to be on my own to watch it. I shook my head reluctantly, wishing I could be strong enough to say yes, but knowing I didn't want to be on my own – not when I was still feeling so jumpy. Jack did his best but it wasn't the most comfortable evening I've ever spent. His guilt was palpable as was my animosity and the shadow of Iona hung over us both.

It probably had nothing at all to do with the fright I'd had, but at my next appointment with the midwife, my blood-pressure was raised enough to register some concern.

'Especially with your history,' she said, and that one sentence repeated to Jack was enough for him to insist, quite forcefully, that I give up work right away and for me not to argue. The midwife had already suggested that it would be the sensible thing to do, especially as I was already within the time scale to be able to start claiming maternity pay.

'The money isn't even important.' Jack looked at me as if I was mad when I mentioned the latter. 'How can you even think about it?'

No, the money wasn't important to him because he had obviously convinced himself that our future lay together in this house, in spite of what had happened. Every penny was important to me because I wasn't convinced of anything beyond the here and now.

I didn't put up much of a fight – in fact, I wasn't even sorry to leave, because with the job becoming ever more stressful, the office wasn't my favourite place to be – though the thought of being at home alone was less than appealing if I was being honest. Whether I would ever go back and pick up where I had left off remained to be seen, though I was assured that the door would remain open for me to return at the end of my maternity leave.

'You know how much we think of you,' Peter said, adding softly, 'how much *I* think of you.'

Yes, I did have a very good idea of how much Peter thought of me. I had always known and a part of me was really sorry that I couldn't return even a little of that regard. He was the nicest of men, pleasant, if non-descript in the looks department, being tall and thin with short grey hair and pale blue eyes. Though I didn't have to remind myself that looks weren't everything, I wasn't attracted to him in the same way he obviously was to me. I liked him very much, but like was lukewarm compared to what I had always felt for my big, blond Jack – and might even someday feel again.

'I'll say no more,' Peter continued, 'except to remind you that you have my contact details and, should you need me, I will *always* be there for you – and for your child.'

I was touched and even a little bit shocked because, despite realizing that Peter had feelings for me – you can't work closely with someone for such a long time without being aware of such a thing – this was the closest he'd ever come to an out and out declaration of the way he felt about me – and how little regard he had for Jack, though his reasons for that dislike were unclear to me. However, he had never over-stepped the mark and I knew he never would. He was far too much of a gentleman for that.

I would have been a liar if I didn't admit – even to myself

– that a part of me wasn't tempted by what was clearly an offer. Life with Peter would provide me with a safe haven for me and my baby and the security that had been missing since the discovery of Jack's affair – and if the excitement was missing, well, I felt I'd had enough excitement these past few months to last me a lifetime. I said none of this to Peter. I had never encouraged him in any way and I wasn't about to start now, no matter what the circumstances.

My team arranged a hasty leaving party for me at work, taking me out to lunch and all signing a huge card and putting into a collection that resulted in a gorgeous baby changing unit filled with everything a newborn might need. It made the reality of the arrival of a real live child very hard to ignore but, for my own peace of mind, I still felt that I had to because, despite the fact the due date was just around the corner, I was all too aware that there was a lot that could still go wrong. I had been disappointed too many times in the past to just relax and enjoy my pregnancy and, anyway, relaxing wasn't an appropriate word for anything about any part of my life since Christmas day.

When I spoke to Jack about the possibility of returning to work he simply said there was no need at all to be making decisions about the future at this stage. I wasn't entirely sure if he was talking about the job or about us, but I was too tired to think about it.

After the initial novelty of not having to get up at the crack of dawn every day to join the rush hour traffic in the bumper to bumper journey to the other side of Brankstone, it took only a very few days with my feet up to feel ready to climb the walls with boredom. I was only too pleased to eventually start venturing out on gentle walks round the nearby park with Betty and her trio of dogs. Gemma appeared to have adopted me as a deputy mistress and so it was her lead I always volunteered to hold.

As I left home to join Betty on my second day out, I bumped into the black-haired neighbour coming to my front door carrying the rake.

'Hi,' he smiled, and I had to admit he looked quite normal, despite his overlong black hair, and nothing like Iona close up. 'Just returning the rake – it was good of your husband to allow me the loan of it. We've had quite a bit of work to do in the garden since we moved in, and I don't have all the tools I need, which is why I've had it so long. I hope I didn't startle you the other day, only he did tell me that it was in the shed and to just come round and help myself.'

'Not at all.' I shook my head and smiled, and we both carefully ignored the matter of the hurriedly slammed door and bolts being shot speedily and quite noisily into place.

'I'm Tom,' he said, holding out a hand to shake mine. 'Me and my wife are quite new to the neighbourhood – though I did grow up here – and first impressions were that people round here weren't very friendly. Your husband – Jack, isn't it? – changed our perspective of that. He even mowed the patch of grass in our front garden after he'd finished Mrs Bramshaw's.' He nodded a little bashfully in the direction of my bump. 'When's the baby due?'

'I'm Fay, and the baby is due in May,' I said, crossing my fingers superstitiously behind my back.

'Ours is three months old now,' he said proudly. 'A little boy. His name's Oliver and he's a little belter. No doubt you and my Julie will be pushing your prams to the shops together in the near future.'

The blood had almost stopped in my fingers because I was crossing them so tightly, but I managed to smile again and murmur as if in agreement, before adding, 'I must go.' I nodded to where Betty and the dogs waited patiently for me out on the pavement. I could see that Gemma was pulling to get to me.

'If you wouldn't mind just propping the rake next to the side gate, Jack will put it away when he comes home.'

'He seems very nice, doesn't he?' Betty waved merrily to Tom as we set off. 'So nice to have another young family living in the road, the babies can grow up together.'

Why was everyone so determined to ignore the fact that my baby wasn't safely here yet, I wondered, as I realized that my fingers had automatically crossed again in my pocket. Or was I actually becoming more paranoid instead of less the closer it got to my due date? The truth was that as the months passed I couldn't bear to think about all the things that could still go wrong and was forced to acknowledge that it had stopped me from ever sitting back, just enjoying my pregnancy, and looking forward to the birth as I should.

My non-committal 'Mmm' must have alerted Betty to the fact that all was not well in my world, and she gave me a long, hard look.

'You're not still worrying, are you, Fay?' She didn't need to clarify what I might be worrying about because the pregnancy was always uppermost in both of our minds. She also probably understood my concerns better than most because, as a midwife, it had once been her job to deal with her patients' worries.

I shrugged, and muttered, 'I know I'm being silly.'

'You are *not*,' she said firmly. 'It would be a miracle if you didn't worry after all you've been through in the past and really, there is nothing any of us can do or say that will make you worry less.'

'No,' I agreed, grateful for her sensitivity and understanding.

'Are you afraid of actually giving birth?'

'Not of the labour itself, only of what can go wrong during childbirth,' I admitted. 'I couldn't bear to get that far, go through the labour and still leave the hospital with my arms empty. Yet that's all I seem able to imagine, probably because it's all I've ever known. Why can I never picture myself holding a happy, healthy child?'

'Because that's something completely outside of your experience,' Betty suggested.

We stopped and let the dogs off their leads, watching them amble off together like three old women on a shopping expedition. If one showed a bit of interest in a particular bush, the other two would go over to check it out, and I noticed how they grouped together whenever another dog approached. They obviously realized they were stronger together than apart.

'You might be right,' I agreed thoughtfully. 'I have no nephews or nieces, and we stopped seeing friends who had children so long ago that if I ever held a baby I don't remember it now. I know there are no guarantees and that's what frightens me. Birth seems a very precarious business to me.'

Betty smiled. 'I could quote you statistics that should prove to you that childbirth is safer today than it's ever been, but I have the feeling that if I said ninety-nine per cent of women in this country give birth without a single problem you would just remain convinced that you would be in the remaining one per cent. I'm right, aren't I?'

I pulled a face. 'I'm that transparent, am I? Yes, I know I am. I would love to be able to enjoy every moment of the one pregnancy I've ever experienced that has at least a reasonable chance of reaching a successful conclusion – but I can really only appreciate this minute of this day, because I know how swiftly things can change.'

'Have you talked your concerns and fears over with your midwife?' Betty asked.

I nodded. 'Oh, yes, she's been wonderful and has had the patience of a saint with me, but she can't give me a solid assurance that I will be safely delivered of a living child and if she did, I wouldn't believe her. Look, the girls are coming back already.'

The three dogs were trotting towards us at a fairly nimble pace. Given that they weren't known for speed-walking, I was already aware this was a fairly rare occurrence.

It was Betty's turn to nod. 'Oh, yes, here they are. I didn't think they'd want to be out for too long because they particularly wanted to see *The Alan Titchmarsh Show* today. The Barking Blondes are going to be on offering tips to pet owning viewers.'

I was intrigued, as I always was with Betty's dogs and their TV viewing habits. 'Do you mind telling me how you know that – never mind how the dogs can possibly work out what they want to see?'

'Because the TV guide is on the coffee table with the programme highlighted,' she told me quite seriously, and then she burst out laughing at my amazed expression. 'That's for me, of course, because none of them can read, but they are creatures of habit and they aren't often wrong or disappointed with their choice of viewing.'

'What do they do if you want to watch something they aren't fans of?' I had to ask.

'They turn their backs on the TV and go to sleep.'

We were both laughing as we clipped leads to collars and made our way home.

'I know it's not easy for you,' Betty said, resuming our earlier conversation as we paused by her gate, 'but do try and relax a little. Tension isn't good for the baby or for you. You should perhaps start thinking of packing a case for the hospital – putting the baby's clothes together might help you to picture him or her wearing them.'

'Maybe.' I said it to make her happy, but I knew I wouldn't be able to do it – I was far too superstitious.

I watched with a smile on my face as Betty disappeared into the house with her impatient dogs pushing against each other to see who would make it through the door first behind her. I almost jumped out of my skin as a voice suddenly spoke behind me.

'Hi, you must be Fay. Tom was telling me about you.'

I turned quickly – too quickly – and suddenly feeling giddiness sweep over me, I had to grasp the pillar that supported the garden gate and close my eyes for a moment.

'Oh, I'm so sorry. I didn't mean to startle you,' Julie – I remembered her name was – said and, abandoning the pram she was pushing, she came and helped me to sit on the wall. 'I should know, of all people how light-headed you can get during pregnancy. I fainted in the middle of the supermarket with my trolley piled high when I was carrying Oliver. Mind you, when I came round they couldn't get my shopping through the checkout and loaded into my car quickly enough, so it wasn't all bad.' She laughed so merrily that I couldn't help joining in.

She came to sit beside me, pulling the pram so that it was right next to her and putting on the brake.

'Not long for you by the looks of it.' She indicated my bump and, without waiting for an answer, continued chattily, 'Soon your peaceful existence will be a thing of the past.' She nodded towards the pram. 'Don't let the silent moment fool you – it will soon be shattered because his feed is due any minute and you can set your clock by him.'

As if to prove her right, vague stirring noises could be heard coming from the pram, quickly followed by a little whimper that reminded me of the mewing of a cat.

'What did I tell you?' Julie pulled a rueful face. 'It doesn't take long to get to bellowing pitch, so I'd better get on. Pity, I was hoping we could get to know one another.' I think she noticed me peering nervously at the pram and, probably mistaking my apprehension for interest, she encouraged, 'Have a peep if you like, you won't disturb him.'

I risked the quickest glance and just caught sight of the top of a tiny head covered with downy hair of a non-descript hue.

'He's beautiful,' I said, backing hurriedly away as a loud wail emitted from beneath the pram hood, adding, 'and hungry.'

Grasping the pram handle, Julie went to walk away and then stopped and turned back to face me. 'Why don't you come in with me?' she invited. 'It won't take me long to get Oliver changed and fed, and then we can have a lovely chat over a nice cup of tea.'

I wanted to say 'no' more than anything, the refusal was right there on the tip of my tongue, but there was something about her invitation and something about the look on her face; she was smiling a bright smile. She hadn't added a please to her request, but I was aware of it hovering there between us like a silent plea.

'Just five minutes then,' I relented, even though it was the last thing I wanted to do. I purposely hadn't been around a baby for years, because it only reminded me of every loss I'd suffered, every child I'd carried for so brief a time and the heartbreak that followed. I was all too well aware that now wasn't a good time to be reminded of my unhappy past, or of what the future might still hold for me.

My reluctant feet dragged as I trailed behind Julie to her front door, I even helped her to lift the pram inside. Then I carefully looked everywhere but at her as she lifted the by now screaming baby into her arms and made her way to the staircase.

'Make yourself at home,' she urged. 'I'll just change him and will be right back down.'

'Shall I make the tea?' I offered, desperate for something – anything at all – to do.

'That would be wonderful.' She beamed over her shoulder. 'You'll know where the kitchen is because these houses are practically identical in design – though I'm sure your house is far more up-together than this one is. We have a lot of work to do.'

She was talking all the way up the stairs, but then she disappeared from sight and I stood looking around. I couldn't remember who had lived in the house before – terrible to acknowledge that, especially when I did recall that they had lived there for a good many years. It was an older couple if I really thought about it and the inside of the house reflected that because the décor was dark and old-fashioned, and made me glad of the light and airy feel of my own home.

I found my way to the kitchen which was also dated and in desperate need of a facelift, but the walls had been painted a pretty primrose yellow in an obvious effort to brighten it up. It was just a pity the units were so dark.

I found a tray, tea pot and mugs quite easily and while I was waiting for the kettle to boil, I heard Julie come back down the stairs and go into the lounge. The baby was still crying, but not quite as loudly, and very soon he stopped altogether.

I was taken aback when I carried the tray though to find that she was breastfeeding and wondered why I'd been so quick to make the assumption her baby would be bottle-fed.

'Oh, sorry to come barging in.' I hesitated in the doorway. 'Would you rather I waited in the kitchen?'

She laughed. 'I don't mind if you don't. You're talking to someone who has absolutely no qualms about feeding her baby in Costa Coffee or Starbucks on a busy Saturday afternoon. I can make myself totally oblivious to any tutting behind my back, because making sure my baby is happy is more important than the approval of a few small-minded people.'

I came right in and placed the tray on the coffee table. Once I was sitting in the chair opposite, there was no avoiding looking at the baby and I stopped trying after asking myself if I really intended to stare at the ceiling for the duration of the feed.

'Are you going to breastfeed?' Julie asked, easing the baby from her swollen breast in order to bring his wind up – which he did very promptly and with gusto. 'Takes after his father,' she grinned, and we both laughed. 'So are you a breast or bottle fan?' She nodded down at the baby who was once again tugging furiously at her nipple. 'I decided breast was best because not only is it best for baby, but it saves making up all those feeds.'

'Erm, I really don't know,' I admitted, 'because, to be honest, I still have trouble picturing myself even holding a baby, never mind making decisions about feeding one.'

'Because of your previous experiences?' she asked softly, and I could only nod, wondering why Jack would share such information with people we didn't even know. He was usually more private than that.

'I can understand that.' Julie lifted the now sleeping baby from her breast, wiped a dribble of milk from his mouth, and tucked him expertly into the Moses basket beside her. She must have noticed my doubtful look because she continued. 'Perhaps Jack didn't tell you we had to go through IVF several times to get Oliver. The last time was definitely going to be the last time because we had no more money to continue paying for treatment and no chance of getting more. I couldn't believe it when I discovered I was pregnant, and I couldn't relax and enjoy the pregnancy until Oliver was safely here. Even now I check his breathing a hundred times a day.'

At last, *at last*, there was someone in front of me who understood my feelings about my pregnancy exactly – even though our problems came from a slightly different perspective. While Julie's problem was obviously that she couldn't get pregnant, mine had always been that I could, but had never managed to carry a baby to full term.

I'd had sympathy of all kinds over the years, but never from someone who truly knew what I was going through and could share my pain and fear. I burst into tears and when Julie took me into her arms, she did the same.

Chapter Thirteen

'THAT'S WHY TOM and Julie can't afford to do the house up yet,' Jack explained, after I'd told him about the visit to our neighbour and the confidences Julie had shared with me. 'The older couple that used to live there are Tom's parents and they gave the house to Tom and Julie when they moved into rented sheltered accommodation. They would never have afforded a house of their own otherwise, not with all their money going on IVF. Now the baby is safely here they're hoping to get started on some DIY eventually.'

'Why didn't you tell me about them?' I demanded and knew I sounded accusing.

His tone was patient as he explained, 'Honestly, Fay, I didn't know a single thing about them until Tom asked to borrow the rake and, understandably, you weren't in the mood to listen after he'd frightened the life out of you. The black hair isn't his real colour, by the way. He works in a bank by day and is an Elvis impersonator by night – he'll do anything to bring in the money, he says. Of course, that means Julie spends a lot of time without adult company, though it also means she can stay home to look after their baby. Like us, they've waited a very long time for a child of their own.'

I gritted my teeth and just stopped myself from saying I appreciated that they had, but for us, the waiting wasn't yet over, and only Julie seemed to grasp just how worrying the waiting was – which was unsurprising given her past. In fact, the closer I came to my due date the more worried I became, which seemed ridiculous even to me, but I was just far too aware of all that could still go wrong and I tormented myself daily with various frightening scenarios. I was pretty sure Jack wouldn't understand.

I would have loved nothing more than to go mad and rush out to buy everything a new born baby might need, but I was far too superstitious. I had done nothing to start preparing for the baby – except for that one trip to Mothercare, and look what had happened that day.

I had heard somewhere quite recently that it was unlucky to bring the pram into the house before the baby was born and that had frightened me so much that, seeing the state of me, Betty had offered to take even my few Mothercare purchases home with her. I hadn't even dared to so much as look at a pram, cot or Moses basket since – not even online.

It was as if Jack read my mind, but with a total lack of any understanding of my fears – irrational though they may be – because he suddenly said, 'Don't you think it's time to start making preparations for the baby's arrival, Fay? We're almost into May now and the little book the midwife gave you advises you should have your bag packed ready for going into hospital by this point.'

My first reaction was to wonder what the hell he was doing even reading the book, when it was *me* who would be giving birth. My second was to fly off the handle and argue what I knew perfectly well was a minor point.

'I think you'll find,' I snapped coldly, 'that it says to have it ready two weeks before the due date.'

'Yes, I realize that,' he started to say, extremely unwisely I thought, 'but with your hist—'

'If one more person brings up my bloody history,' I fumed, 'I shall bloody well explode. I am well aware of it, Jack, after all, I'm the one who went through the heartbreak of numerous miscarriages, and I really don't need reminding that thus far every single one of my pregnancies has failed to produce a living, breathing baby. Having it continually and unnecessarily pointed out hardly instils confidence in me and my ability to complete this pregnancy successfully – as I thought you might have understood.'

Jack looked stunned for a moment, and then he said, 'But this time is *completely* different. There can't be any doubt that you're carrying a healthy baby – the scans have clearly shown that the baby is developing just as it should. There is absolutely no reason to suppose that anything will go wrong at this late stage. And you seem to be forgetting, Fay, that though it's undoubtedly true that you were the one who was pregnant, those babies also belonged to me, and I went through the heartbreak each time with you.'

It was my turn to be stunned because he spoke nothing but the truth, but I was in no mood to be reasonable. 'Oh, yes,' I said, most unfairly I was aware, even as I was saying it, 'and then it was you who went off and found consolation in someone else's arms and, in doing so, put what is probably our last chance of having a child together, in jeopardy.'

Jack opened his mouth to speak, to say what, that he hadn't known I was pregnant, that she wouldn't take no for an answer? Whatever it was, I didn't want to hear it and turning on my heel, I stormed from the kitchen where the exchange had been taking place, and out of the house.

I was shaking when I turned up on Betty's doorstep, but more from anger than cold, because it was a mild enough evening.

'You've got to stop all this,' Betty told me sternly when I had given her a garbled account of the latest altercation with Jack.

I had been so sure of her taking my side that I was completely taken aback and stared at her before asking, 'What do you mean?'

'All this stress is not good for you and it's not good for the baby.' Betty sounded more severe than I had ever heard her. 'You have to stop dwelling on a pregnancy history that clearly isn't relevant in this case, and you also have to stop dwelling on an affair that is also history. I thought you two were making a go of your marriage, pulling together for the sake of that little mite in there.' She swept a hand towards my bump. 'But instead you are close to allowing that awful woman gain the upper hand.'

'But ...'

'You should be enjoying your pregnancy, my love. Focussing on the best outcome, not the worst, and also making the best of your relationship with Jack for now, even if in the end you decide to part at some time in the future. Why not try,' she said, 'living for today, leaving the past behind and letting tomorrow take care of itself.'

My first instinct was to turn right around and march back out of Betty's house the way I had marched out of my own, but something made me stay.

I finally admitted, 'I'm just too afraid to give in and accept that what will be, will be and that there's very little I can do about it.'

'So you'd rather spoil each day that comes along by

worrying about the next,' she smiled gently at me, 'even though you know in your heart that worrying won't change a thing.'

'When you put it like that ...'

I popped in to say hello to the girls on my way out. They were, as ever, sitting in front of the TV, engrossed in *The Chase* on this occasion, though Gemma immediately came over, pushed her nose into my hand and then looked up at me adoringly. Zoe and Sadie barely gave me a glance.

'So, is Bradley Walsh on their list of favourite presenters?' I couldn't help asking.

'Oh, yes, they're very fond of him,' Betty told me, without hesitation or humour, 'but they prefer the woman out of the different Chasers and, as you can see, she's on today.'

I found that I was still smiling when I went indoors, to find that Jack was standing exactly where I had left him. I went straight over and put my arms around him, remembering as I did so that it was probably the first time I had voluntarily touched him more than briefly since ...

I stopped the thought even as it started and looking up into his face, I said, 'I'm sorry.'

He was clearly completely taken aback. 'You have nothing to be sorry for, Fay. It's me ...'

'You can't keep telling me you're sorry for the rest of your life, any more than I can keep punishing you for the rest of mine. If you tell me that it's over, then I have to believe you, and learn to let it go. I doubt I will ever forget, but I can and will try to forgive.'

Jack's arms came round me and drew me closer. We stood like that for a while and it felt good. We'd been through so much together over the years and I finally realized it would be madness to throw it all away just as our dreams of a child of our own were about to come true.

When he placed a finger under my chin and tilted my face to his, I thought he was about to kiss me – and I knew I wasn't ready for where that might lead – but he just said, 'Thank you, Fay. I know I behaved like a complete idiot but you have my solemn promise that I won't let you down again.'

There was an awkward moment when neither of us seemed capable of making the first move to pull part, and then we laughed a little self-consciously as we disentangled our arms.

'Food,' I cried, a little too heartily. 'I'm a heavily pregnant lady and I need feeding, but I never switched the oven on for the casserole and it will take far too long to cook now. Fish and chips?'

'Nah.' Jack shook his head. 'Let's go out. The carvery down the road will have quietened down after the teatime rush, let's go and treat ourselves to a roast that someone else has cooked.'

We walked arm in arm and that felt good, too. I found I was actually starting to see the truth in needing to let my anger go, because clearly it was hurting me more than anyone else.

We were quickly shown to a table and in no time had joined a very short queue and were helping ourselves to heaped plates of meat and potatoes, not to mention lovely, freshly cooked vegetables from the carvery. We tucked straight in and didn't talk much while we were eating, but the silence between us felt really quite comfortable.

'This has been really nice,' Jack said, wiping his lips with a serviette and placing his knife and fork neatly side by side on a plate that had been cleared of all but a few smears of gravy.

'Yes, it's lovely,' I agreed, spearing a last piece of crispy roast potato onto my fork.

'I wasn't just talking about the food,' he said, and his smile was quite shy. 'This – us – you and me.'

I found myself smiling back and agreed, 'Yes, I know.'

'Fay, how are you?'

I looked up to find Peter Lucas standing by the side of our table, looking from me to Jack as if he couldn't believe his eyes. He'd clearly either heard a rumour or I had said more than I intended to on my last rather emotional day at work. I couldn't think now – his sympathetic nature, dislike of Jack and obvious fondness for me were no excuse – and I felt my face burn. He must wonder what I was doing enjoying, what was obviously a cosy meal, with my adulterous husband for all the world as if the disastrous past few months had never happened.

Pulling myself together with a determined effort, I said, 'You remember my boss, Peter Lucas, don't you, Jack?'

Jack stood up quickly, smiling and holding out his hand. Peter looked at it as if it was something nasty scraped from the bottom of his shoe for a long moment, before he finally took it and shook it with an obvious show of reluctance. Peter then turned back to me so swiftly that his action couldn't be taken as anything but the snub to Jack that it was.

'So, how are you?' he asked again.

I had to remind myself that my personal life and my personal choices had nothing to do with Peter – whatever details I had, rather foolishly, seen fit to share with him.

I lifted my chin, looked him in the eye and said, 'I'm very well indeed, Peter, as you can see.'

He took my hand then, and looking into my eyes, he said, 'You know where I am if you need me, Fay,' before walking away without another look in Jack's direction.

'You told him, didn't you?'

'I think I must have let slip that all was not well with us,'

I replied, without apology. 'I guess he caught me at a weak moment.'

'The guy is in love with you,' Jack said, without rancour and simply stating what he saw as a fact.

'Is he?' I stared at him, quite shocked. That he liked me I already knew, that he might actually love me was something very different.

'Mmm.' Jack nodded, adding, 'And who can blame him? He clearly thinks I'm an idiot – and who can blame him for that, either?'

'Let's forget him because in the scheme of things, he really isn't important. Now, where is that dessert menu because I think I can manage a little taste of something sweet.'

Nothing – I decided, as I enjoyed the last of my sticky toffee pudding while Jack went off to pay the bill – nothing, was going to change my resolve to take Betty's advice about living for today – and today had been pretty good in the end, all things considered.

To say I was totally unprepared for Iona to suddenly materialize next to the table was a massive understatement, and it was all I could do not to gawp foolishly up at her.

'Can I help you with something?' I said at last, thankful that my tone was absolutely steady, not to mention icy cold. 'Only it appears that you have lost your way.'

I couldn't have spoken truer words because to say Iona didn't fit into the family eatery's vaguely scruffy surroundings was another massive understatement. Dressed up to the nines, the heavy make-up on her face immaculately applied and with not a hair out of place, she stood out like the proverbial sore thumb. People were looking, probably wondering if she was some sort of celebrity; all that was missing was the oversized sunglasses. I only just stopped myself from looking for the paparazzi entourage.

'Oh, no,' she said with a knowing smirk, 'it's you who have lost – you just don't know it yet.' And she paused for a moment before she added, 'But you will – oh, yes, indeed you *will*.'

With that she spun on her ridiculously high heels and the next minute she was gone.

I looked over to where Jack was stood in a queue, still waiting to pay and, realizing he wouldn't be aware of what had just happened, I resolved to keep it to myself. The woman was obviously a poor loser, just as I had known from the first minute I set eyes on her, and far too used to getting her own way. I took a few deep breaths, determined not to let her sudden appearance rattle me or to prompt me into arguing with Jack – which would have been my normal reaction. To do so would be playing right into Iona's beautifully manicured hands, just as Betty had so rightly pointed out.

I was quiet as we made our way home, and I caught Jack looking at me curiously once or twice when my responses to his efforts at making conversation were monosyllabic.

I made a firm effort to force all thoughts of Iona out of my mind and, making a decision that was – for me – momentous, I found myself saying, 'Time is getting on and I think we should start making all the necessary preparations for the birth of this baby, Jack.'

'Really?' Jack stopped in the middle of the pavement and, spinning me round to face him, he kept his hands on my arms so that we stood face to face. He looked absolutely thrilled. 'You're quite sure?'

I nodded, and he kissed me shyly and very gently on the lips before releasing me.

'We have to get absolutely *everything*,' I said with emphasis, 'because the few clothes I bought and even the changing station from the girls at work are a mere drop in the ocean.'

'Everything except the pram.' Jack was as aware of that superstition as I was, and we smiled at each other before turning towards home again.

'We'll have to decide which room will make the best nursery,' I mused out loud, 'and we can order all the big stuff online to make life easier.' I indicated my eight month pregnancy bump with a rueful grin. 'Probably we shouldn't have left it so late – but that's my fault, I know.'

Jack pushed his key into the lock and opening the door, he ushered me inside. 'Before we start looking at catalogues,' he said, 'I think there's something I should show you.' And taking my hand he led me up the stairs, stopping outside his office door.

I stared at him mystified as, with a very nervous smile on his face, he turned the handle, opened the door and gently pushed me inside and I found myself standing in a beautifully decorated and fully-equipped nursery.

Chapter Fourteen

THE ROOM HAD been transformed. Gone was the dark grey carpet, the mahogany desk and the matching filing cabinets, gone the masculine wallpaper and Jack's framed accountancy certificates, and in their place was a bright, light room, the plain lemon walls were brightened with a Winnie The Pooh border, matching lamp shade and several bigger characters hung on the walls here and there. A white cot had been erected and made up with white bedding and the changing station stood ready for action in the corner.

'I thought our baby should know from the start how very welcome he or she is,' he said, still looking at me nervously as he waited for my reaction. 'I couldn't tell you before because ...'

'Yes, I know, and I do absolutely love it, Jack,' I said, and then bursting into noisy tears, I asked him, 'but what would you have done if something had gone wrong?'

'Then you would never have seen the room looking this way, but this time – especially when the scan showed that the baby survived your nasty tumble unscathed – I felt certain that nothing would. I accepted from that day that this baby was here to stay no matter what.'

'How did you do it – the decorating, the furniture and everything, without me guessing what you were up to?'

'Well, I used the excuse about touching up the paintwork to hide the fact that I was decorating and I made sure you were at work when I brought the furniture in. I tried to be as quiet as I could when you were at home and after ... you know, you never came in here.'

He was right. I hadn't been in this room once since Christmas day, I hadn't even bothered to come in and clean. Before that, I would often pop up when Jack was working – with cups of tea and coffee, the odd sandwich and snippets of news to share.

'But where will you work now? You didn't have to give up your study, there are other rooms,' I pointed out.

'None of them would get the sun in the morning, and none were just the right size or the right proximity to our – your,' he corrected himself very quickly, too quickly, 'room.'

'Just give me time,' I told him, 'please. I can only take one small step at a time.'

'I know,' he agreed, with a rueful smile.

I went into that bright little room every single day after that, sitting in the nursing chair which was another addition that Jack had thought of, and trying hard to imagine myself taking care of our baby in the nursery he had so lovingly prepared. It was completely against my cautious nature to take anything for granted, but I kept reminding myself that Betty was absolutely right – I *should* be making an effort to enjoy the last weeks of my pregnancy because it was almost definitely an experience I wouldn't be given the chance to repeat again in the future given my age and, yes, my history.

'You've come this far, little one, and there is just one more journey – your birth that we must face together before you're out into the world safely and in my arms,' I said out loud, spreading my hands around my baby bump and feeling a reassuring kick against my fingers.

'I have no idea how or why you've been spared – the one precious child who has managed to hold on in there – but I swear you won't regret it. You have a mummy and daddy waiting to give you all the love in the world. I completely understand that you can't be the one to heal the damage between us, but because of you we may be able to make the effort needed to heal ourselves.'

I never told Jack, or even my mother or Betty about Iona's sudden appearance in the restaurant, trying not to place too much importance on it, but I did share it with Julie.

'What a strange woman,' she said with a grimace. 'Obviously a poor loser and just out to cause trouble.'

'That's what I thought,' I agreed. 'I don't think she's dangerous but I'm not an idiot and will carry on taking sensible precautions, like keeping the doors locked and the windows closed when I'm alone. However, I can't be kept a prisoner in my own house. I rarely go out on my own, but I can't expect my mum and Betty to always be available either. An occasional trip to the shops in broad daylight can't do any harm, surely?'

'I'll walk to the shops with you,' Julie offered immediately. 'I always go on my own and it would be great to have some company.'

I hadn't actually meant I wanted to go right at that very minute, but Julie looked so keen that I didn't have the heart to say so.

'OK,' I smiled, 'but best wear a mac and carry an umbrella because it's only just stopped raining.'

'And I'll put the rain-cover on Oliver's pushchair before we leave because it can be a bit of a nightmare if you're trying to do it in a downpour. I won't be long. Pop and get your coat and we'll see you out the front in five. The fresh air will do us all good.'

I pulled on the loose raincoat my mother had loaned me, to avoid the expense of something I would wear only occasionally, and wondered which shop in the precinct I could say I wanted to go to and what I could pretend I was going there for exactly.

It soon turned out that I needn't have bothered wondering, because Julie had already decided we weren't going to the precinct at all, but to the newly refurbished high street in the original part of Brankstone. It was a part of town that time had forgotten until quite recently when some property developer, who had apparently grown up in the area, had swept back into town to give it a much needed facelift. It had been much publicized in the local press, but I hadn't seen the improvement for myself.

'I know it's a tidy step,' Julie said, 'but it's not *too* far and, if you do find it a bit much we can always catch a bus home. I really love it there. It's not as big as the precinct and is much less impersonal with lots of little specialist shops – fabulous for browsing, but I'm probably preaching to the converted and you've been there loads of times.'

'Actually, I haven't there in years,' I admitted. 'What with working and everything there's never the time or the inclination. We've always tended to shop for most things at one of the out-of-town superstores or online because it's so much quicker. I never have been one for meandering round shops before so this will be a whole new experience for me.'

'You're in for a treat,' Julie assured me.

Chatting away about this and that as we walked, we

covered the distance in no time. The rain had stopped and a watery sun was just starting to peep through the clouds and it felt good to be out. When we reached it I couldn't help being impressed with the new look high street, which I vaguely recalled from one long ago visit as being very shabby. The majority of shops had boarded up windows and, of the rest, charity shops had far outnumbered local traders. It was a visit I had never felt inclined to repeat and only now – thanks to Julie – I was finally seeing just what I'd been missing.

I hadn't done much reading lately but, even so, found myself drawn to a bookshop that also sold fantastic cards, by some woman who was quite well-known locally so the big man serving behind the counter told me and, although my mum's birthday wasn't until July, I couldn't resist buying the one I found with exactly the right words inside. As I told Julie with a grin, I was just hoping I would remember where I'd put it when the time came around. Then I found a book of baby names and I couldn't resist that, either. Names were something Jack and I hadn't even begun to discuss, but choosing names we both liked was obviously very important. I found I was looking forward to us perusing the book together.

We bought fresh bread from the baker who proudly told us he baked everything on the premises daily, then fresh fish from a fishmonger who was very knowledgeable regarding what was especially good for a pregnant woman and what should be avoided.

'Wonders have been worked on the sad little high street that I remember,' I said, and Julie agreed.

'One more stop,' she said, 'and then we'll have a cuppa in the little tea shop down there.' She pointed along the street and then, peering into the pushchair at the sleeping baby added, 'Oliver will probably be ready for his feed by then, but first you have to see this. It's my favourite shop – for obvious reasons. What do you think?' she asked coming to a sudden stop and pointing.

I found myself standing in front of a baby-wear shop that – judging by the window display – sold all the beautiful little outfits that were rarely found in bigger stores selling mass produced, more practical outfits. I eyed up the frilly dresses with matching sunhats and tiny shoes side by side with miniature sailor suits, and was suddenly overcome with the urge to know whether I was carrying a little girl or a little boy – despite my determination all along not to know.

Once inside, I resisted the urge to buy at least one of each of the outfits from the window, but chose some gorgeous little sleep suits that would do for either sex. Then I surprised myself by ordering a beautiful Moses basket lined with white broderie Anglaise, which would be delivered the following day, and enjoyed a feeling of excitement no longer tinged with fear.

I joined Julie in poring over half a dozen little summer outfits that would fit Oliver as we came into warmer weather. There were so many to choose from and she was still undecided when Oliver started fretting and, when the whimper quickly became a roar, I offered to push him along the street while she made her choice and purchases.

'That would be great,' she said gratefully. 'I had to leave in a hurry last time I was here for the same reason, so it would be fantastic to actually get the chance to buy something today.'

I steered the pushchair carefully through the shop doorway and out onto the pavement. With the motion Oliver stopped crying almost immediately. I wandered slowly along, looking into shop windows and, enjoying the unusual experience of steering a stroller, finally allowing myself to feel confident that it would soon be me pushing my own baby and even permitting myself to feel a real thrill at the thought of the pleasures to come.

'You've had it, then.'

Where on earth had she come from? The bloody woman seemed to have developed a knack of suddenly appearing from nowhere. Determined not to be intimidated, I would have just kept walking but Iona had planted herself right in front of the pushchair and, mindful of the sleeping baby, I refrained from barging her out of the way.

'Does Jack know it's not his?' she demanded.

I didn't dignify her outrageous question with a response, merely requested quietly, 'Get out of my way, please.' Iona didn't move and I hadn't been expecting her to.

'You do know he only stayed with you because he was sorry for you, don't you? The trouble with Jack is that he's too nice a person to leave you pregnant and alone.'

I couldn't let that go and, raising my eyebrows, said coldly, 'As opposed to the likes of you, who would steal a pregnant woman's husband without a second thought?'

'Oh, I didn't have to steal him,' she sneered, 'I can assure you that he was very willing – and he still is. If you think our affair is over then you're even more stupid that I took you to be.'

That hurt, as of course it was meant to, because I had to accept that there just might be a remote possibility that she was telling the truth, but I kept my gaze steadily on her and when Iona looked away, I was as certain as I could be that she was lying.

'What is it, then? Boy or girl?' She stepped to the side of the pushchair and peered through the rain-cover.

'Jack didn't tell you, then?' There was derision in my tone, because we both knew how unlikely that would be if they were actually still seeing each other. The fact she obviously didn't know that this baby wasn't even mine, either, spoke volumes to me and was further proof – if I needed it – that the affair really was well and truly over.

'It's a boy,' I said firmly, 'and he's the absolute image of his father. Now why don't you just go away and get a life, Iona, preferably *not* with someone else's husband.'

With that, I wheeled the pushchair forward so swiftly that she had to jump back pretty nimbly to avoid having feet, encased as they were in their expensive shoes, run over. I kept walking, without a backward glance, intent only on putting as much distance as possible between us.

'Hey, you're in a hurry – *and* you've gone straight past the tea shop.' Julie was completely out of breath so she must have been hurrying to catch up with me for quite some time. She took one curious look at my face, and demanded, 'What's happened, Fay? Because obviously something has. You're as white as a sheet, and look.' She took my hand in hers. 'You're shaking.' A glance at the still sleeping baby told her that all was fine there and she came back to me, her gaze searching my face.

I shook my head, quite unable to speak.

'Come on,' she guided me back to the café and ushered me inside, pulling the pushchair in behind us and setting off towards a table at the rear. When we were seated and tea had been ordered, she turned back to me again. 'So come on then, are you going to tell me what just happened out there? Something definitely did.'

'It was her. Jack's mistress – ex-mistress,' I corrected myself firmly. 'I was walking along pushing Oliver and minding my own business, and suddenly there she was. She blocked the pathway or I'd have just walked on. She thought Oliver was my baby.'

Julie threw a surprised look in the direction of a baby bump that was quite substantial now and pulled a face. 'Really? You're kidding me. Not very observant, is she?'

I managed a wry smile, and then said, 'She assured me she is still seeing Jack.'

'And do you believe her?' Julie poured us both a cup of tea and put mine into my hand, urging, 'Drink up, Fay. I've put plenty of sugar in yours because you've obviously had a bit of a shock.'

I sipped, grimaced and said, 'It's like syrup.'

'Drink it,' she ordered.

I sipped obediently, and found the warmth was comforting, because I was still shaking even though I didn't feel particularly cold. Looking back, I was amazed at how calmly I had managed to deal with Iona, because I certainly didn't feel calm now.

'I might have had my doubts *if* Iona hadn't been so certain that Oliver was mine. You're right that she can't be very observant because Mum's mac isn't *that* baggy. She even asked me what I'd had – as if Jack wouldn't have told her if they were still seeing each other. I did tell her that the baby was a boy and he looked just like his father – that much was true at least – and she came right back to insist the baby wasn't Jack's, which was also true because Oliver isn't.'

'I wish I'd been there,' Julie said, narrowing her eyes.

'She would never have approached me if you'd been there, Julie,' I assured her, 'she's obviously far too astute to ever come near me when I'm with someone. She doesn't want witnesses to her actions or words.'

I went on to put Julie completely in the picture, including the shop-lifting episode and the fact that seeing Tom in the shed with his long black hair had freaked me out.

'Iona has long black hair, you see,' I explained, 'and she did appear inside my house once. She'd stolen Jack's key to let herself in.'

Julie was horrified. 'I think you should go to the police,' she said firmly, picking Oliver up to breast feed him beneath a strategically placed muslin nappy. 'The woman is obviously deranged.'

'That's as maybe, but she's also clever enough never to have any witnesses so there's no proof.'

'What about the woman who saw her put the item in your bag—' Julie started to suggest.

'She was elderly,' I interrupted, 'and could easily have been mistaken, and all the other small things, if examined, would look like nothing more than coincidences and just be impossible to prove.'

'Fair enough, but you must be careful, Fay. I don't like the sound of her, and I really feel we must all be extra vigilant. There's just no telling what she might do next.'

I would have liked to pooh-pooh what she said, but her words were too close to what I was feeling myself. The thought of what Iona might be capable of sent a shiver down my spine and for the first time I actually felt really afraid.

Chapter Fifteen

I TRIED HARD NOT to become paranoid but, after the last little altercation in the high street, it became ever harder not to expect Iona to appear around every car parked in the street or from behind goods displayed in the shops. Common sense told me she wouldn't come near because my mother, Betty – once they had been alerted – and Julie as well, stepped up their protection programme. In fact, I could hardly move for them. Acting as my personal bodyguards, they always made sure at least one of them was with me whenever I left the house – with Jack taking zealously over at weekends.

It was clear he was mortified that as a direct result of his ill-conceived affair, I was under some kind of threat. I confess I wasn't as understanding as I might have been simply because there was no doubt that he *was* to blame for my present circumstances. It didn't help at all to remind myself that he hadn't known he was getting involved with a mad woman, because the plain truth was that as a married man, he shouldn't have been getting involved with anyone – end of story.

Another thing that didn't help was being made to feel even more like a prisoner in my own home, especially when April turned into May and the weather warmed up – making it perfect for sitting outside in a garden that I no longer felt safe to enjoy.

'You're never going to forgive me, are you?' he asked sadly when, once again, he came home from work to find me fuming indoors with the house locked up because everyone was too busy with their own commitments to come and babysit me.

I ignored him for several moments while I waddled round the downstairs rooms, throwing open the doors and windows to let fresh air and sunshine into the stuffy house. He was still waiting for an answer when I came back to where he was standing in the hall.

'I am trying,' I told him, and then shrugged. 'But it is hard when I have to be reminded every bloody day of the effect *your* mistake has had upon *my* life and, think about it, Jack, is it going to get any better after the baby is born? I'm going to be even more paranoid then, aren't you?'

Jack looked stunned, as well he might I thought bitterly, when he was being reminded that his unhinged paramour might turn out to be a threat to our much wanted baby.

'I'm going to the police,' he said suddenly. 'This can't go on.'

'But—'

'No buts.' His tone was firm. 'Even if they can't *do* anything, they need to be made aware – and they may have advice about what we can do, other than keep locking you away to keep you safe.'

In the end, I reluctantly agreed and even said I would go to the police station with him, though I hated the thought of discussing Jack's sordid affair with strangers because I felt – wrongly or rightly – that I would be judged for not being able to keep hold of my own husband. They would probably lump the pair of us together and say we had brought this on ourselves. Sometimes I thought it might have been easier if Jack *had* left me for Iona. At least then she would have no further interest in me personally.

'We need to take with us all the notes we've made about actual and possible happenings – starting from her appearance in this house.'

Then I found myself in the position of having to tell a horrified Jack about Iona's appearance in the restaurant.

'And you didn't think to tell me about it?' He was furious.

'What good would it have done? You were paying the bill and didn't even notice. She did nothing except spout her usual load of drivel and by the time you came back she was gone. She may even have had a legitimate reason for being there. It was a public restaurant, after all, and I presume she does live somewhere in the area.'

We were still arguing the point when my mother suddenly swept in through the open back door and, with her first words, took the wind completely out of our sails.

'I've been to the police,' she stated baldly before she had even taken her coat off, 'and then I thought it best to come straight here in a taxi to tell you what they said.'

We stared at her open-mouthed.

'You did what?' Jack said finally.

'Went to the police,' she repeated, 'and don't you look at me like that, Jack Ryan. Someone had to do *something* about this ridiculous and extremely worrying state of affairs. My daughter is eight months pregnant and is being made to feel like a hostage in her own home. With her history ...' She paused when she caught my look and then continued determinedly, 'Yes, with your history, Fay, you are extremely vulnerable. The stress you've been put under all this time could have proved fatal for that precious child and maybe even for you. It's time that woman was stopped once and for all.'

We stared at each other and neither of us could find a reason to disagree with what she said.

'I didn't actually report the bloody woman, but only because I didn't feel it was my place and it's not actually *me* she's bothering,' she advised us. 'I just gave them all of the facts as I know them, and asked for their recommendations.' With that, she pulled a sheaf of papers from the depths of her handbag and spread them out across the kitchen table. 'They strongly suggest that you both pay them a visit as soon as possible because they believe you may have a strong case for harassment against this Iona.'

'Oh.'

I knew that I sounded surprised. I must admit I had thought the police would simply dismiss a sorry tale of a nuisance ex, when they would obviously be dealing with far more serious things on a daily basis, but I could see from some of the literature in front of me that they were providing us with lots of advice on ways of dealing with what really did amount to serious harassment – according to the information.

'See what it says here.' I pointed to what I thought was a particularly relevant section, and then read it out word for word.

'"Whilst there is no strict legal definition of 'stalking', section 2A (3) of the PHA 1997 sets out examples of acts or omissions which, in particular circumstances, are ones associated with stalking. These include: physical following; contacting, or attempting to contact a person by any means (this may be through friends, work colleagues, family or technology); or, other intrusions into the victim's privacy such as loitering in a particular place or watching or spying on a person.

'"The effect of such behaviour is to curtail a victim's freedom, leaving them feeling that they constantly have to be careful. In many cases, the conduct might appear innocent (if it were to be taken in isolation), but when carried out repeatedly so as to amount to a course of conduct, it may then cause significant alarm, harassment or distress to the victim."'

'There,' said my mother in the satisfied tone of someone who knew for certain her recent actions had been completely justified, 'you can't have it any clearer than that. The woman is breaking the law – actually breaking the law – and she could find herself in very serious trouble. Anyway,' she continued and I wondered what more was to come, 'until the matter is dealt with in an appropriate manner and that woman officially warned off, I will be moving in with the pair of you – at least until the baby is safely born.'

With that, she nipped outside the door and when she came back she was wheeling a fairly substantial suitcase behind her.

For a long moment we just stood and stared at her, and then as I felt the relief flood through me, I realized that this was just what I wanted and needed. I burst into tears and launched myself into her arms.

'Thank you, oh, Mum, thank you.'

'Yes.' Jack finally smiled and looked happier than he had been for a long time. 'You are just what we need right now – the perfect solution.'

It wasn't until we were halfway through supper that I thought to ask. 'How did you get round the back of the house, Mum?'

My mother stared at me. 'The side gate was unlocked,' she said, 'in fact it was half open, and I thought coming round the back would save you from answering the front door.'

'No,' I said, very quietly, 'the side gate *wasn't* unlocked

172

– I'm very certain of that.' And I felt the blood freeze in my veins at the thought of Iona peering into my house – and of the awful shock I'd have received had we come face to face through one of the window panes.

Without another word I added one more item to the growing list we would be providing to the police – because I think we had all finally accepted that we could no longer deal with this on our own.

'I think we're stirring up a hornets' nest,' I admitted nervously, 'though, I do realize she's left us with very little choice. I think we must accept that Iona will probably become very angry with me if we go to the police.' I looked up from the list to admit something that was really bothering me. 'Because I'm definitely the one she will heap all the blame onto – and I'm a bit fearful about how that anger will manifest itself.'

'But she has to be stopped, Fay,' my mother said. 'This can't go on, surely you must see that.'

Jack picked up one of the sheets we had been looking at earlier and after another quick glance he waved it at us. 'Look,' he said, 'it says here that if you don't want to take action through the police, you can go to a solicitor and obtain an injunction through the civil courts. Perhaps that would be a better way to deal with her.'

'That's going to cost,' I said.

'I don't care,' he replied firmly. 'Your mother is right, Fay, she has to be stopped. I'll fit a padlock to the bolt on the gate tomorrow first thing, and make an appointment with a solicitor. I'm also going to see what I can find out about her from the branch she worked at previously. I know there were rumours and I have contacts in other areas. I'm sure people will talk willingly enough because she wasn't always popular with everyone.'

I didn't sleep well, tossing and turning, and dreaming that I was being chased by a faceless woman with long black hair that streamed out behind her, and in my arms I carried a new born baby.

'You look so tired, my love,' my mother commented when I arrived in the kitchen the following morning. 'Didn't you sleep well?'

'Not very, no.'

'We will get this sorted out, Fay, I promise you. I should have taken action a lot sooner and I'm sorry I didn't,' Jack said, adding, 'you really don't need this right now.'

I managed a smile. 'It's not all your fault,' I told him. 'Like me, you probably thought she would eventually just go away.' I pulled a face. 'She obviously thinks you're quite a catch.'

'God knows why,' he muttered.

As it was a sunny day, my mother and I decided to get to work in the front garden, getting the borders ready for bedding plants. Working in the open, we felt, would be the best way of letting any interested party know that I wasn't on my own – Betty and the dogs soon joined us and then Julie and Oliver. Several other neighbours stopped to pass the time of day, but of Iona there was no sign. I hadn't thought there would be, but I was sure she was out there somewhere, watching us. Though with her surveillance programme taking up so much of her time, I did find it in me to wonder how she ever got any work done.

Jack popped back briefly to fix the padlock and a sturdier bolt onto the side-gate and to advise us that he had made an appointment with a solicitor for the following day. A little research had also revealed the name of someone he knew well at Iona's previous place of work, and he was planning to make a very carefully worded phone call.

174

In the afternoon, after we had tidied ourselves up, my mother and I went into town in order to buy the various items on the list of things that I was going to need for my hospital stay.

'It's really going to happen, isn't it?' I looked at her as we made our way from the car park to the precinct and felt a little bubble of excitement as I added, 'I'm really going to have a baby.'

My mother looked at the thrust of my belly and laughed. 'Oh, I don't think there's any doubt about that. Now where shall we start?' She became business-like. 'Where's that list?'

We ended up tittering as we tried to work out what size of bra I would be requiring after the birth and, in the end, had to take advice from a knowledgeable sales assistant.

'Will you be breastfeeding?' she asked, and I felt very stupid admitting that I hadn't given it a thought, though she didn't seem that surprised. Perhaps there were other women out there like me who – even at this late stage – still couldn't quite believe they were about to produce a real live baby and what they were going to do with it when they did.

The list seemed endless, but most items could be purchased from the same shop and we worked our way through it with the kindly assistant's help. I wondered if she was on commission, and hoped so because she had more than earned it as far as we were concerned.

'I'll take these bags back to the car,' my mother said, refusing to allow me to carry even the smallest and lightest. 'I won't be long.'

Remembering all too vividly the time I was out with Julie in the high street and what had happened the minute we had parted, I said immediately, 'I'm coming with you.'

'You don't need to do that, Fay, I won't be more than two

ticks.' She smiled and then, perhaps noting the way I glanced nervously around, added, 'oh, I'm so sorry, my love, how stupid of me. I clearly wasn't thinking. Come on, we'll walk back together – it really isn't that far.'

We turned to make our way to the car park and almost bumped into Peter Lucas, who appeared to have stepped out of the nearby bookshop, though there was no sign of a purchase.

'Fay,' he said, sounding delighted, 'how are you?'

'As you see,' I said, grinning and indicating my bump, 'I'm very well. This is my mum, Iris.' I pulled her forward. 'I'm not sure if you two have ever met. Peter Lucas was my boss, Mum.'

We exchanged pleasantries and then Peter suggested, 'Can I treat you both to a coffee of tea? Or are you in a hurry?'

'Actually,' my mother said, looking pleased, 'that would be great. You can look after Fay for me while I take these bags back to the car. It'll save her an unnecessary walk and I won't be long.'

Peter placed his arm lightly round my shoulder as he ushered me into the nearby Costa Coffee establishment. He quickly found a table, and helped me into my seat as if I were a delicate flower, then went back to the counter to place an order for tea all round.

'So,' he said, when he came back and had set the tray of tea on the table, 'do you need looking after then, Fay, as your mother seemed to indicate? Everything all right at home?'

A truthful answer would have been 'not exactly,' but I had told him rather too much already and didn't want to encourage him in case he was harbouring any lingering ideas about the two of us getting together. He was old enough to be my father and, anyway, I wasn't yet at the point of totally discounting a future with Jack if we could iron out our difficulties, put the past behind us and make a home together for our baby.

'Everything is *fine*. Jack and I have put our problems behind us and are both looking forward to the baby,' I said firmly and then looking up with a smile, exclaimed, 'ah, here's Mum.'

I was eager to hear news of my colleagues at work, though not so keen to hear how well they were managing without me. Peter did add that I was greatly missed – I hoped it wasn't an afterthought. Though to be fair I had to admit, if only to myself, that I hadn't missed working at all. In fact, the only thing I had missed was the stress that went with a responsible job and Iona had filled that gap rather too well.

I cursed myself for allowing her to creep into my thoughts and spoil what had been a very pleasant day so far. I tried, and failed, to stop myself from peering at the occupants of the other tables nervously. Thankfully, I could see no one remotely resembling my husband's glamorous black-haired ex-mistress. It would be nice to think she had given up and gone away.

I forced myself to concentrate on what Peter was saying – something about a book he'd been unable to find and the bookshop staff not being very helpful. He probably hadn't even noticed that I wasn't paying much attention, what with my mother hanging on his every word.

'You should try the one in the high street,' I told him. 'I was in there the other day and they couldn't have been more helpful, going out of their way to find what I wanted.'

'Really?' Peter looked doubtful. 'I thought the high street was a tatty place, full of charity shops and empty ones with boarded up windows. I can't imagine finding a decent bookshop there.'

'That's what I thought, too,' my mother was quick to agree, 'I never go there anymore.'

'Well, you're both wrong,' I told them firmly. 'It's all been beautifully refurbished, but not in an ugly modern style, and is full of little family-run businesses and speciality shops. You should try it.'

'Well, I will,' Peter assured me. 'In fact, I should be getting back, so I'll go that way. Thank you for the recommendation.'

We all got up to leave and Peter bade us goodbye on the pavement outside, kissing us each on the cheek in his gentlemanly way and hoping he would see us again before too long.

'What a lovely man,' my mother exclaimed. 'It's not often you meet such a gentleman.'

She went on in the same vein as we made our way back to the car, and in the end I asked her laughingly, 'Smitten, are you, Mum?'

'No,' she denied immediately and emphatically, and then she giggled in a very girlish way, and admitted, 'well, I might be – just a little bit, you know. He *is* very nice, isn't he?'

'*And* he's on his own.' I grinned, and we both laughed.

None of us were laughing the very next morning when an envelope addressed to Jack arrived by special delivery. Inside were several photographs of Peter and I in the café, looking very cosy with our heads apparently close together. Others had been taken outside where the camera – angled just right – managed to make a simple kiss on the cheek look like a full on mouth to mouth lingering one right there in the street.

A post-it note was attached on which was scrawled in black capital letters the message, 'YOUR WIFE AND THE FATHER OF HER BASTARD CHILD GETTING UP CLOSE AND PERSONAL. WHAT MORE EVIDENCE DO YOU NEED THAT <u>SHE</u> (heavily underlined) IS THE ONE CHEATING ON <u>YOU</u>?'

Chapter Sixteen

JACK HAD OPENED the envelope in the hall after he'd collected the package from the postman after first signing for it, but the minute he came into the kitchen he spread the contents on the table there. We stood staring down at the photos. If it wasn't so freaky to think she had been right there watching me share what was so obviously nothing more than an innocent cup of tea with an old friend, it would have been funny – but neither of us was laughing now. We were long past finding any of this amusing.

'She must be getting absolutely desperate now,' was all I could find to say. 'Those pictures were taken in a busy café and on a crowded street with my mother standing next to me – only she was just out of shot, of course. I'm beginning to appreciate how celebrities must feel and I can tell you I don't like it. I don't like it at all.'

'If I had any doubts about seeing the solicitor,' Jack said, his expression grim, 'I have none now. This is past a joke.'

'What is?'

My mother breezed into the kitchen, freshly showered and obviously ready for the day ahead. She was brought up short by the sight of the photographs and note on the table, and she went from smiling to snarling in seconds.

'*This*,' she snapped, 'has gone too far, Jack, and it's high time you stopped talking and did something about it. *You* started this with your shenanigans and *you* have to be the one to put a stop to it once and for all. What the hell were you thinking? That's what I'd like to know? Wasn't my daughter enough for you? It was thoughtless – thoughtless – to start an affair with no consideration given to the possible consequences....'

I'd never known my mother so articulate, and she looked set to continue for quite some time. Jack just stood there with his head hanging, looking more and more humiliated and ashamed, taking everything she was dishing out to him without offering even one word in his own defence.

'That's enough, Mum,' I said quietly but firmly.

'Yes, but...' she protested, 'if he...'

'I said that's enough. I know you mean well, but you're not helping or saying anything I haven't already said ages ago. It won't improve matters in any way if we start tearing lumps out of each other.' Noting the relieved look on Jack's face, I turned on him. 'But that doesn't mean that I don't agree with her words, even if you have heard them before, mind.'

'Shall we have a more thorough look through the information the police provided me with?' Mum waved the sheaf of papers that had been left sitting on the side.

When Jack sat down as well, I stared at him and asked, 'Shouldn't you be leaving for work?'

'I have the morning booked off,' he said, reminding us, 'for the appointment with the solicitor. Going through this might help us to prove we have a case for an injunction against Iona. It would certainly clarify for me exactly what constitutes harassment or stalking.'

I was shocked. 'Can what she's been doing actually be described as stalking then?'

'Yes,' he said seriously, 'I really think it can. Perhaps you'll go through and read out the relevant bits, Iris?'

My mother shook out the papers and cleared her throat importantly. '"By definition,"' she began, reading straight from the first sheet, '"Stalking is defined as a constellation of behaviours in which an individual inflicts upon another repeated unwanted intrusions and communications (Mullen, 1999). Intrusions include making approaches, maintaining surveillance and gathering information." Well.' She looked up. 'I think that covers just about every single thing she's done or is doing, don't you?'

There was a lot more – about taking action against the perpetrator because ignoring the harassment wouldn't neces-sarily mean it would stop – which was exactly what we had been doing in the hope that Iona would just get fed up and go away. It clearly hadn't worked. The information also stated that you shouldn't respond to the person, but that was almost impossible when she always caught me unawares and was often standing right in front of me. Letting everyone around me know what was happening was something I had done, and I felt a bit better knowing we'd got *something* right, as we had also done with making a record of every incident.

Being told – even on paper – that I wasn't overreacting was kind of liberating, because it was stated clearly that if you felt scared, worried or angered by the behaviour of the other person then you shouldn't have to put up with it. It also said that stalking without violence was still damaging and could cause severe psychological distress to the victim, and that victims should always remember that the problem is with the person doing the stalking/harassing and not with themselves.

'Well, I feel vindicated after all that,' I said.

My mother and Jack both stared at me as if I was mad.

'None of this is *your* fault nor has it ever been, Fay,' my mother insisted. 'Why on earth would you think it is when – from start to finish – you haven't done a single thing wrong?'

'But I always have had the feeling that I could or should have handled things differently right at the beginning – you know, when she was here, standing in this house.'

'Like what?' Jack asked, looking confused. 'She was totally and utterly in the wrong even then. Taking my key like that and coming into my – our – house and walking around as if she owned the place. I should actually have phoned the police right then.'

'Yes, you should,' my mother reacted angrily to his words.

'No,' I contradicted her, 'he shouldn't. How could Jack possibly have known that her odd behaviour was going to continue? None of us could have. All along we've dealt with it in the best way we knew how and given her every opportunity to stop what she was doing. I really don't think that – even in her delusional state of mind – Iona can blame us for putting matters into the hands of a solicitor at this point. Do you?'

My mother harrumphed and said, looking straight at Jack, 'Well, I think you're being far too kind to people, Fay, who don't deserve even the tiniest bit of your kindness.'

Jack left soon after to keep his appointment. We had decided he should go alone to the initial consultation, because I had an appointment of my own with the midwife and, anyway, he could put forward all the evidence without my help. There was also the fact that I really didn't want to have to sit and listen to all the sordid details of Jack's affair. I had the feeling that if I knew too much about it, I would find it very hard to *ever* forgive him – and against all my original feelings – I found I did want to give our marriage another chance if it was at all possible. At the moment we were struggling by one day at a time, but I was hoping that would change once the baby was born.

'What's suddenly changed your mind?' I asked my mother when Jack had gone. 'You were the one championing his cause at every opportunity from the very beginning – telling me in no uncertain terms that Jack should be given the chance to make amends.'

'Well,' she said, her tone harsh, 'I didn't know then that it was going to turn out like this, did I?'

'To be fair,' I told her, 'none of us did – least of all Jack.'

'Putting you in danger,' she went on, as if I hadn't spoken, 'and causing all this stress. It's a miracle that little baby in there has survived – especially given your—'

'Yes, Mum,' I interrupted, 'you don't have to remind me, but this baby is obviously on a mission to be born safe and sound, and I'm also on a mission to make absolutely sure that he or she is.'

My confident words were echoed by the young midwife. 'Baby's head is engaged, so when baby decides it's time, we're all set for the natural birth you've set your heart on.'

'Mmm.' I smiled. 'It will almost definitely be my one and only experience of childbirth and I intend to enjoy every moment of it – if "enjoy" is the right word for labour.'

'Pain relief is available and you'll be carefully monitored from start to finish,' she assured me.

My mother had something to say about natural births in general and what she thought of that idea, particularly in my case, immediately after the midwife had left but luckily, Betty soon arrived and showed herself ready and willing to fight my corner.

'A caesarean section, Iris,' she told my mother in no uncertain terms, 'shouldn't be seen as an easy option – though I know it often is these days. It is a major operation and should only be contemplated when absolutely necessary. Let your daughter enjoy the rest of her pregnancy, Iris, and the birth she wants at the end of it.'

My mother looked chastened, but she still said firmly, 'I was only thinking of Fay and the baby and what would be best for them both.'

'Of course you were,' Betty agreed readily. 'But the hospital is well aware of Fay's pregnancy history and will be prepared for any eventuality. They do know what they're doing.'

'You're right,' my mother allowed, and then she sighed. 'I'll just be glad when it's all safely over.'

'Look,' I said, in an effort to change the subject, 'it's a gorgeous day out there. Why don't we take a walk to the park? We could take the dogs with us if we can tear them away from Philip Schofield. What do you think, Betty?'

'I'll go and see what they think.' She made for the door, saying over her shoulder, 'It will depend a lot on what guests they have on but I'll see if I can persuade them.'

My mother gave me a bemused look. 'She talks about those animals as if they're real people. Does she really believe that her dogs can possibly be that discerning about their TV viewing?'

'"Those animals",' I said sharply, 'are Betty's family and to her they are "real people". You should go round and observe them watching TV sometime, and then come back and tell me they aren't picky about their viewing. I've regularly seen them turn their backs on programmes they don't like. They look so disgruntled that it's hilarious.'

In the event, Betty's 'girls' were waiting happily at the gate with her, tails wagging eagerly, and she offered the explanation for their willingness to walk while *This Morning* was still on as the fact there were too many reality celebrity guests on the programme that morning.

'They're not at all keen on *TOWIE* stars, though I don't mind them – especially that Joey Essex. If I'd ever had a son I'd have liked him to be just like that young man.'

My mother's expression was quizzical, but she said nothing. She was a staunch soap fan herself and watched very little else. I thought it was just as well that she didn't have a pet with the set preferences that Betty's dogs had, and grinned to myself at the thought of her owning a cat or dog who tried in any way to influence *her* TV viewing.

I knocked on Julie's door in case she felt like joining us, but there was no reply so I relieved Betty of Gemma's lead and we set off. It really was a gorgeous day and the trees in the park were covered in blossom. I didn't have to try too hard to picture myself on a day like this, pushing my baby proudly along these paths and taking the little one to the swing park at some time in the future. It was something I never thought I would be lucky enough to experience and my heart swelled with joyful anticipation.

Betty's girls even stirred themselves enough to chase a ball across the grass, each dog vying to be the one to carry the trophy back proudly to Betty's feet and receive her warm praise.

'This will do us all good,' my mother said happily, picking the ball up and preparing to throw it before she became distracted and carried on talking. 'Almost makes me want to get a dog myself. I don't exercise nearly enough, but there are enough places to walk near me and I can see how it would help me to make friends, too. Every dog-walker we've met so far seems to know Betty and even her dogs – all three of them – by name.'

'Oh, yes,' Betty agreed readily, 'almost without exception, dog-owners are a friendly bunch, and they're out here in all winds and weathers, too, always someone to walk with and chat to. Yet most of us wouldn't venture outside of the door on wet days if it weren't for our dogs.'

Gemma sat patiently by my side, but Zoe and Sadie were sitting directly in front of my mother, eyes bright with anticipation, mouths agape and tongues lolling, making it look very much as if they were laughing.

'Mum,' I said, pointing to the dogs.

'Oh.' She looked at them and then at the ball in her hand. 'Are they waiting for me to throw it?'

Betty and I both nodded, and then watched as my mother threw the ball with all her force – straight into the thick foliage of a nearby clump of Rhododendron bushes. The two dogs took off like rockets, barking as they went, and we carried on walking slowly, knowing they would soon catch up when one of them found the ball. However, shortly afterwards when they caught us up, panting heavily, of the ball there was no sign.

'Wait there, I'll go and see if I can find it,' I said and set off.

'Oh, don't worry,' Betty urged, 'it's only a cheap tennis ball. I have others at home.'

'I'll just have a quick look,' I called over my shoulder.

It wasn't far and I quickly arrived at the edge of the bushes, poked around a little and then, finding nothing, stepped further into the leafy bower, my gaze scanning the ground for the yellow ball.

There was no yellow ball to be seen but, quite suddenly, I was brought up short because there was a pair of shoes in my

line of sight. They were of a type that looked totally incongru-
ous in this setting, being sharply pointed and stiletto heeled,
not to mention bright red in colour.

'Are you looking for this?'

Of course, I knew who the shoes belonged to even before
she spoke and I looked up slowly and into Iona's cold grey
eyes.

Chapter Seventeen

MY FIRST THOUGHT was to question my own stupidity in forgetting the safety in numbers ruling that we had all been so meticulously applying in order to avoid just this very scenario. I wanted to turn and run – run as far away from this weird woman as I could get. I *wanted* to run, but seemed totally incapable of moving so much as an inch.

My second thought was to recall the advice my mother had read out that very morning that under no circumstances should you try and talk to the person harassing you. However, it was advice that could be more easily followed on a busy street or over the telephone, but less simple when the person in question was standing right in front of you and you were both tucked away out of sight. However, so far I had managed to remain silent.

Iona held out the ball again, and I noticed with vague satisfaction that the mud from it had spread onto her beautifully manicured hands and under the blood red nails.

'Go on,' she said her tone cold with dislike and distain, 'you can take the ball from me, but,' she added, 'don't think for one minute that you can take Jack away from me. We're soul mates, we belong together, and there's nothing you can do about it.'

It was too much, this calm certainty of hers that it was me stopping Jack from being with her, and suddenly all thoughts of the good advice not to respond to her taunts flew out of the window.

'All this time,' I told her, meeting her scornful gaze steadily, 'I have done *nothing* to keep Jack with me – that has been entirely his own choice. In fact, I threw him out at one point and he *still* didn't come to you.' I paused to let that piece of information sink in. 'Oh, didn't you know that? He's a free man, free to go wherever he chooses and with whomever he chooses. The fact that he *hasn't* chosen to be with you all this time surely must be telling you *something*. He doesn't want you, Iona, it really is as simple as that. '

'You're lying,' she hissed, but I could have sworn I saw a brief flash of uncertainty in those cold grey eyes.

Perhaps unwisely I decided to push on. 'Am I? Am I really, Iona? I think you need to ask yourself why he might be seeking a solicitor's advice at this very moment on taking out an injunction against you. Stalking and harassment are arrestable offences, you know.'

'You're *lying*,' she said again, raising her voice.

I knew immediately I had gone too far, especially when she took a step towards me but, before I could move or make a response in any way, there was a low growl. I looked down to find Gemma standing close by my side. Gone was the gentle-natured Lurcher with soft brown eyes, who I could have sworn wouldn't have it in her to so much as hurt a fly. In her place was an animal I scarcely recognized, one with lips pulled back in a snarl, displaying fangs that wouldn't have looked out of place on a wolf living out in the wild.

'Keep that – that thing away from me,' Iona ordered, but I could tell she was shaken, especially when she backed quickly away from me and my four-legged protector.

'She's just taking care of me,' I said, putting a light hand on Gemma's collar when she continued to emit a low warning growl, all the while with her gaze fixed on Iona. The dog obviously knew when someone she loved was being threatened and I was so grateful for her comforting presence even while I was wondering if she really was capable of attacking someone.

'You can't win, Iona. Surely you realize that, after all these months. Jack has made his choice and – unfortunately for you – *it isn't you*. If he had chosen you I can assure you that you would be very welcome to him.' I didn't add that if the shoe were on the other foot she should have been thinking similar thoughts, but I could tell from her expression that I was getting the message across. 'All you are going to gain from continuing to harass me is a day in court, a criminal record and a reputation lying in ruins. I would advise you to think about that carefully.'

I felt I'd said all there was to say on the matter, and I turned and walked away. When I glanced back there was no sign of Iona – it was as if she'd melted silently away.

'Oh, there you are.' Suddenly my mother was there peering anxiously between the leaves.

'We wondered where you'd got to,' Betty joined in. 'Are you all right? We were getting worried.'

I stepped out of the shade and into the sunlight, and shivered in spite of the warmth of the day, as I said, 'Iona, she – she was there, in the bushes, waiting for me.'

'Oh my God.' My mother put her hand up to her face, her horrified gaze meeting mine over the top of her fingers.

'She didn't touch you – hurt you?' was Betty's reaction as she stepped past me and peered into the undergrowth.

'No, and she's gone now. Gemma helped drive her away.' I

managed a weak smile.

'Gemma?' My mother's tone was incredulous. She'd never been much of a fan of Betty's dogs. For all of her talk of getting one, I could tell the attraction of owning a dog was lost on her.

'Oh, yes. You should have seen her. Snarling and giving Iona the evil eye. Maybe she wouldn't have attacked, but she certainly gave a very convincing performance of being a dog that was about to. She definitely gave Iona something to think about.'

'Well,' Betty looked surprised and pleased. 'I can't say she's ever been put to the test before, but being given a hint of what she might be capable of will certainly help me to sleep more easily in my bed at night.'

'Are you all right, Fay?' my mother asked, full of concern.

'Actually,' I said, and I even managed a smile, 'I think I'm better than all right. I think this time I actually got the message across loud and clear that Jack doesn't want to be with her. If he wanted to be, he would be, it's as simple as that and so I told her. She didn't like it very much.' I almost smiled at the huge understatement, 'but I'm sure if she was ever honest with herself, she would have already worked that out. I also told her he had gone to see a solicitor about taking out an injunction against her.'

'Oh, but Fay, didn't it say in the information not to communicate with the stalker in any way?' Betty looked worried because all the advice had been discussed with her, too.

I shrugged and told her, 'Yes, you're right, Betty, it did – but I defy *anyone* not to respond when they are being as severely provoked as I was. I'm sick of being accused of keeping Jack from her. It might have been the wrong thing to do but, thanks to my guardian angel here ...' I stroked Gemma's smooth head and she looked up at me adoringly, once again the gentle dog I had come to know and love. '... I came to no harm – and I might even have done a bit of good. At least I've given Iona something to think about.'

We walked slowly home, with Gemma close by my side all the way and, with Betty's permission, I popped into the local butcher for a nice piece of fillet steak for her tea. I was well aware the meat would be shared between all three of the dogs, but as long as Gemma got her fair share I was more than happy. In my eyes, she deserved a medal for her performance, but she would probably prefer sharing the steak with her friends.

The minute we turned into our street, we saw Julie hurrying towards us, pushing Oliver in his buggy.

'She's been here – in the street,' she told us without preamble and, without pausing for breath she hurried on. 'At least I think it was her, though I've never actually had the dubious pleasure before, but with her height, the long black hair and done up to the nines, she stuck out like the proverbial sore thumb.

'What happened was that I caught sight of her out of my bay window. She seemed to be just hanging around out on the street and, guessing who she was, I was horrified. I came out to ask her what she wanted but, by then, she was further up the street talking to that nosy Miss Curtis. You know, the woman who's always cleaning her front windows and brushing her path so she can see what going on. Then Oliver started to cry and I had to go back indoors to see to him, and when I came out again, they had both gone. I was just on my way to come looking for you. Did she...?'

'Find us?' I nodded and Julie looked absolutely appalled, so I quickly reassured her, 'But no harm done. If you've got time to pop in for a cup of tea, we can tell you all about it.'

We took it in turns to dandle Oliver on our laps as the story was told, mostly by me – since I was the one in the bushes being confronted by my husband's scary ex-mistress – but with eager input from my mother, and also Betty, who couldn't help showing her pride in the fact that her dog's brave involvement had pretty much saved the day.

Julie's face was a picture, as she went from gasping in horror one minute, to clapping her hands and smiling her approval at Gemma's uncharacteristically fierce contribution the next.

'What's going on here?' We all looked up when Jack poked his head round the door. 'Has something happened?' As he stepped into the kitchen, where we were sitting round the table with tea cups in front of us, we all started talking at once. 'Whoa, whoa,' he laughed, reaching to take an eager Oliver out of my mother's arms, 'one at a time.'

He sat down, accepted a cup of tea – which he had the good sense to keep well out of Oliver's reach – and listened with very evident disgust to the details of my encounter in the bushes with Iona. Then it became clear that she wasn't the only one he was annoyed with.

'I can understand that you were being goaded, Fay, but could you not just have walked away? The solicitor has stated to me quite categorically today that we shouldn't meet or communicate with her *in any way*,' he said, sounding quite put out, 'as it may weaken any prosecution case against Iona simply because it might appear that we have co-operated with her.'

'Yes,' I told him, crossing my arms and glaring at him furiously, itching to smack the self-righteous look off his face. 'Well, that's all right for you to say, isn't it, Jack? *You* aren't the one she is constantly confronting and pestering. It's pretty hard to ignore her or to walk away when she's standing right in front of your face, spouting a load of very provoking rubbish. She's convinced herself that the fact you're still here instead of with her is all down to me, and spends her time telling me – in no uncertain terms – that I should let you go.'

As the conversation between us got more heated, everyone kind of melted away. Julie to get Oliver bathed before bedtime, Betty to settle the dogs in front of Bradley Walsh on *The Chase*, and my mother suddenly remembered something urgent that needed her attention in another room.

The minute Jack and I were on our own, we completely lost it and accusations flew back and forth freely.

I blamed him for the fact the bloody woman was in our lives at all and, for the first time, Jack offered no apology and even refused point blank to accept all of the blame.

'You've never really understood how I felt,' he told me, a savage edge to his tone that was alien to him.

'How you felt about what precisely?' I demanded belligerently.

'About the babies we lost and how that affected me deeply as well as you. As I've said before, I do completely accept that you were the one who carried them and suffered the pain of the physical loss, but I suffered emotionally as well as you. I do wonder if you ever understood the affect those losses had on our relationship – and on me.'

I stared at him, stunned into silence for a long moment, before I recovered enough to demand, 'How has this suddenly become all about you, Jack, and how *exactly* does any of it have anything at all to do with your affair with that blasted woman?'

'She made me feel like a man,' he said simply.

'So,' I said furiously, 'to put it bluntly, you weren't happy with our sex life but, instead of talking to me about it, you found excitement elsewhere. That was a smart move, Jack.'

'You're still misunderstanding,' he persisted, 'and I wouldn't have put it quite like that, but yes, if you must know, our love-making for years had been all about making babies – which of course I wanted as much as you – and even you can't deny that it had definitely become little more than routine once we thought there was no chance of us conceiving.'

'Thanks,' I said dryly, but his words stung because in my heart I accepted they had a hurtful ring of truth about them.

'I never loved her, never cared about her, but I can't deny that it was flattering to be *wanted*.'

I wanted to shout and scream, to ask him how the hell he thought I had felt all those years – feeling like a baby-making machine, and a failed one at that, didn't exactly leave me feeling sexy at bedtime. Then into my mind came a clear picture of me in a hotel room with a man I didn't even know – and then I knew exactly what Jack meant, and I burst into tears and decided that it was time to come clean.

Chapter Eighteen

JACK CALMED DOWN as soon as he saw my tears and hurried across the room to comfort me.

'Look, I'm so sorry, Fay, I went too far and I accept that I should be big enough to admit that the mess we are in with Iona is entirely my fault. There's no doubt at all that if it wasn't for me and my thoughtless actions, none of this business would ever have happened. Please don't cry.'

His arms closed around me and I wanted nothing more than to accept his apology and the comfort he was so generously offering but of course I should accept my share of the blame – if blame was the right word. It was time for some honesty – on both of our parts.

'No.' Reluctantly I pushed him away, but only gently and only so that I could place my hands on his arms, hold him in front of me, and meet his gaze steadily with my own. 'I can't attribute all of the blame to you, Jack, though it's what I've been doing so far. That's just taking the easy way out and I can see now that it isn't going to solve anything.

'It's becoming increasingly obvious to me that vulnerability caused by the extremely difficult circumstances we found ourselves living through has led us to where we are today, with our relationship in tatters, a stalker on our doorstep and yet, miraculously, with the baby we've always longed for about to be born. If we're to stand a chance of happiness together it's time for some real honesty between us, Jack, and then perhaps we can start to move on.'

He stared at me, long and hard. 'You had an affair, too,' he said, and it wasn't expressed as a question, yet there was disbelief in his tone. I could see in his eyes that he really believed I had and that the thought of it hurt him every bit as much as his actual affair had hurt me.

'No, I didn't.' I hesitated, and watched his shoulders sag with relief, but only for a moment as I added, 'Not actually an affair, but I must be honest enough to say that I did come very close to it.'

'Who...?'

'Who was it?' I finished for him. 'No one you know, Jack, and no one at all important. Just as Iona isn't at all important, I can see that and accept it now – apart, of course, from the fact she has given us no chance to even *try* to repair the damage the affair caused to our relationship, because of her persistent attempts to destroy it totally.'

'But you didn't?'

'No,' I replied firmly, 'I didn't, but the whole point is that I *wanted* to, Jack – only for a brief moment – but even the fact that I *almost* gave in to my feelings makes me every bit as guilty as you.'

'Not in my book,' Jack said flatly.

'Well, we'll have to agree to disagree over that but, really, who did or didn't do what isn't really the point. It's the fact that the need was there, that's what's important. It shows that our marriage had gone very badly awry, and now we must find a way to put any anger and ill-feeling aside and talk about what went wrong between us and why.'

Jack nodded, and I appreciated the fact he asked no more questions about my 'not quite' affair and seemed eager to discuss the mess our marriage was in and why that had happened.

'Should we go to the pub, or to a restaurant?' he asked, adding with a nod towards the ceiling. 'Your mother ...'

'And find Iona standing at the bar or sitting at the next table?' I pulled a rueful face. 'I'd rather stay here and have my mother in the next room – at least she's on our side.'

As if on cue, there was a tap on the kitchen door and my mother poked her head tentatively into the room. 'It's quiet in here,' she said, looking from one to the other of us, concern etched on her face. 'Does this mean you've decided to call a truce?'

'Come on in, Mum,' I encouraged, 'you're quite safe.'

Jack agreed. 'We've decided that talking is the way forward, Iris.'

'Just as I told the pair of you months ago,' my mother said severely as she came into the room.

'We weren't ready then. Well,' I amended, 'I wasn't, anyway.'

'Well, I'm pleased you are now, then,' she said, 'better late than never as far as I'm concerned. You two have so much going for you, and not least this little one you've created between you against all the odds. Are you going out? I've heard it sometimes helps to be somewhere neutral.'

'No,' Jack said, 'we thought it better to stay here – if you don't mind us commandeering the sitting room?'

'Oh, don't you mind me,' she said instantly. 'I can make myself scarce, no trouble. But you've not eaten,' she said, and carried on. 'Look, you go ahead, and I'll stay in here and put together a nice salad. Once it's done, I'll go next door and watch the quiz shows with Betty and the dogs.'

'But you hate quizzes,' Jack pointed out.

'I'm sure I shall enjoy watching those three dogs watching the quizzes,' she said, smiling. 'From what Fay's told me, they're an entertainment on their own. I wouldn't be a bit surprised if they have the correct answers sorted out long before the contestants.' She looked at us expectantly, and then encouraged us with a flap of her hands. 'Go on then.'

We went and took our time settling ourselves into the sitting room that I had denuded on that awful Christmas day, months ago, of anything personal. The walls and surfaces were bare of even a single photo of Jack and me together, but I couldn't find it in my head to regret their absence, because that was then and this was now. We had to put the past behind us and that was why we were here, still together, even if it was by the skin of our teeth, and still with the chance of a future together.

There was an awkward silence as we looked at each other, me from my position on the settee and Jack sitting across from me on one of the armchairs. The space between us seemed vast, and for a moment I wondered if we could ever breach it – and then we started to talk.

Our problems, it soon became apparent, went back years, probably to the time of the first miscarriage.

'It happens all the time,' we recalled telling each other, and then immediately went rushing off on one of our many holidays, almost brushing our loss and heartbreak aside.

'Why did we never give ourselves time to grieve for that first baby?' I asked Jack sadly.

He said, 'I just thought you wanted to forget all about it, put it behind us and try again.'

'I thought that was what you wanted, too. You didn't seem

to want to talk about it.'

Looking at each other we began to realize that not under-standing the other's needs that first sad time had probably set the pattern for the difficult years ahead. There had been so much sorrow in our lives that we had never really acknow-ledged or dealt with.

'My mum asked several times over the years if we shouldn't go for counselling and I always told her we were fine and, stu-pidly, I really and truly did believe that we were.'

'Me, too,' Jack said. 'I just thought we were being strong.'

'Yes, accepting so staunchly, as time went on and the preg-nancies failed or didn't happen at all, that we weren't going to have children. It was almost a relief to give up on the tests and fertility charts, wasn't it?'

'I blamed myself,' Jack said suddenly and abruptly.

'Did you?' I was shocked. 'But they did all the tests ... we were told there was no medical reason.'

'I never believed them. I blamed myself and I felt sure that you blamed me as well – even though you never said a single word. I thought you were just being kind.'

I stared at him, seeing from the pain etched on his face that he was telling nothing but the truth.

'But I thought that's how you felt about me,' I said. 'It was how I felt about myself. After all, I was the one carrying – or *failing* to carry – the babies to full term. How on earth could you come to the conclusion that it was somehow your fault?'

'I don't know.' Jack shrugged. 'Something wrong with the quality of my sperm perhaps. Who knows?'

'I can't believe we were both carrying all this guilt, letting it eat into us and spoil what we had together. Oh, Jack.'

'You might not believe it, Fay,' he said, 'but there has never been a moment when I have not loved you. I told the truth when I said I never wanted an affair. I know it's no excuse to say it just sort of happened, but it did and then I didn't know how to get out of it.'

'I can believe that,' I said wryly, 'Iona is a strong-minded lady. I'm quite certain that once she'd set her very determined sights on you that you probably didn't stand a chance.'

'Really?'

'I've seen her in action, remember? She would know exactly the right things to say and do – and catching you at a bad time for us really worked to her advantage. If our relationship had been strong you'd have said no to her, I have no doubt about that.'

'You managed to say no,' Jack reminded me.

I didn't say that, had the circumstances been similar, and the guy had been someone like a work colleague so that we'd got closer over time, I might not have done, instead I said simply, 'But I almost didn't, Jack. It would have been all too easy to say yes.'

'I still think you're just saying that to make me feel better about what I did, and I appreciate that and love you for it,' he said, 'but the question is – where do we go from here?'

I shrugged. 'From where I'm sitting it would seem that we have just one of two choices.'

'And they are?'

'We try to repair the damage we've done – between us – to our relationship.' I gave him a look as I said that, expecting him to argue and, when he didn't, I continued flatly, 'Or we separate.'

Jack was shocked into silence, and then he recovered enough to start to say, 'But what about the ba—'

I interrupted to remind him, 'Staying together for the baby is a really bad idea, and it won't work, Jack, you know that as well as I do. How many couples that we've known over the years have tried to do just that? They all started with the best of intentions, but in the end they were just prolonging the agony. None of them were happy – least of all the children – and separation further down the line was inevitable in almost every case.'

He seemed to think I was saying separation was inevitable for us, because he begged, 'Don't do this, please. I swear to you that I will never cheat again – you can't know how much I bitterly regret it. Please, I'm begging you, give me another chance, Fay.'

I smiled and told him, 'I would like to think there is still enough love between us to make it possible for us to give each other another chance, Jack. I still love you, too, but for a while back there I definitely didn't like you very much at all.'

He grimaced, and said, 'I don't blame you.'

'Well, we've been living like brother and sister for months now and, though that's mostly worked well for us, I'm sure we will both want more eventually, and it may happen – but I think we also have to accept that it may not. We can still share the parenting of our child and make our family work that way, even if we're living apart.'

'Mmm.' Jack didn't sound convinced.

I felt some sympathy for that. It seemed all wrong that our one final chance of living the family life we had always dreamed of should bring with it so many problems. It was also difficult not to think of how different everything might have been if only ... but spending too much time dwelling on 'if onlys' was a futile exercise that resolved nothing and would only build resentment.

'What we have to do, is to learn from our mistakes,' I told Jack, 'and I don't only mean recent ones, but those going back years as well. We have to start with a clean slate and total honesty between us – without honesty we might just as well give up, right now.'

'At least we don't hate each other,' Jack said, and then he stopped and looking straight into my eyes, asked, 'you *don't* hate me, do you, Fay?'

I shook my head, though part of me wondered if I was being entirely truthful. Despite my earlier words about always loving him, I had come pretty close to hating Jack at times, if I was being honest, but then it was a well-known fact that love and hate were just two sides of the same coin.

'Anyway,' I became brisk all at once, 'there's nothing much to be done about the state of our relationship until after Junior comes into the world because – as I keep reminding myself – this *is* your child too – and I really will need your support up to and after the birth. No,' I went on, 'need is the wrong word, I *demand* your support and wouldn't allow you to opt out – even if you wanted to,' I added as he went to interrupt. 'I didn't get pregnant on my own and I don't intend to go through the birth on my own, either.

'However, there is something we can do about Iona and her constant harassment of me, isn't there? You haven't said much about what the solicitor had to say – apart from the fact I should have no contact with the woman who is forever contacting me.'

Jack pulled a face. 'I know, that was a stupid thing to say. I just wasn't thinking.'

'Let's go and eat while we talk some more,' I suggested, 'because I'm actually starving.'

It was a lot to take in, and though Jack shared everything he'd been told very carefully, the facts he presented made my head spin. Since I was the victim of the harassment, it would apparently have to be me who had to fill out a petition for a restraining order and an affidavit that explained what had happened during the abuse situation.

'We need to provide information about Iona's appearance, her home and work addresses, and details of every one of her abusive actions. The solicitor mentioned a photo, too, which I don't have,' Jack said, 'but I know there is one on the company website, which might do. If the judge then accepts your petition for a restraining order, you will receive information about the court hearing within one to two days.'

'But it's not going to happen overnight?' I queried, already knowing what the answer was going to be.

'No, but as the solicitor explained, it doesn't appear that you are in any immediate danger. We just have to continue as we have been, taking care to give Iona no opportunity to get near you.'

My mother returned at that point, and quickly made her very opinionated views on the subject quite clear. In her view, prison was too good for someone like Iona – in fact, being boiled in oil would have been no more than she deserved in my mother's eyes.

'A bit excessive that, isn't it, Mum?' I hid a smile, though I did have quite a lot of sympathy with the strength of her feelings. 'Anyway, telling her that Jack was seeing a solicitor might just be enough to make her think about what she's doing and stop. I did warn her that if she persisted she might well end up with a criminal record.'

'I wish I could take more time off in these last days leading up to your due date.' Jack's tone was regretful. 'But with me so recently starting a new job … They've really been very understanding as it is, but obviously I can't do all of my work from home.'

'Fay's got me here, living right on the premises,' my mother said, adding fiercely, 'and I'd like to see that bloody woman get past me. As you both know, I'm not a violent woman normally, but in her case I might be able to make an exception. The sooner we get this petition signed by you, Fay, the better as far as I'm concerned.'

We obviously didn't need Jack with us for that to be accomplished, and the visit to the solicitor's office the following morning took no time at all. However, though the solicitor went through everything very carefully with us, I still felt as if most of it went completely over my head. I blamed that on my hormones, though my mother wasn't much better but, by the time we arrived home and sat down over a pot of tea to compare notes, we felt we had the gist of the main points.

From what we could remember between us, it would seem that the solicitor presents the petition to a judge and, if he or she accepts it, there would be a court hearing quite quickly. If I didn't attend the hearing, the process would be delayed so I fully intended that I would be present. We were advised that the lawyer could also be in attendance at the hearing, but it wasn't mandatory, though I obviously preferred her to be there and had been very quick to say as much.

I was reminded to bring any and all evidence to support myself, though all I really had to offer was a list of dates and occurrences. I just hoped those details, together with the ridiculous photos and note, would be enough. If the other party i.e. Iona, did not show up to the hearing, the restraining order would usually be granted in their absence. If she did turn up she would be asked to present her side of the story, too.

If, at the end of the hearing, the judge issued a restraining order, it would describe my rights and could last up to five years. If I had to call the police, then the papers would help them to quickly understand my situation and act accordingly. If I lost the restraining order papers, I should contact the court for another copy. The restraining order should clearly state exactly what the other party is not allowed to do, and if these rules are being or have been violated, he or she will be held in contempt of court.

My mother and I sat quoting what we remembered to each other, parrot fashion. What one of us forgot the other recalled, so in the end, it was quite a lot of information and the tea went cold. For the moment, however, we just had to wait and – as my mother reminded me – be very careful to give Iona no window of opportunity to come close to me. There had been a number of times in the past when we obviously hadn't been careful enough, and she had made the most of every single one of them.

I didn't need reminding that, at this late stage in my pregnancy, a face to face confrontation with Iona would be the worst idea possible. In fact, the very thought of even seeing her again made me feel quite ill.

Chapter Nineteen

THOUGHTS OF IONA were far from my mind, however, when I woke after the best night's sleep I'd had in ages to a perfect May morning. Birds were singing, the sun was shining and I was filled with a sense of well-being and, despite my increasing bulk, with far more energy that I'd had for ages. Jack was barely awake before I was ushering him out of the spare room, down the stairs and up step-ladders to unhook curtains.

'I won't have time once the baby is here,' I pointed out, as I busily removed matching cushion covers, 'and look,' I waved an attached label in his general direction, 'these are all washable. I'd like to bet the curtains are, too, so we won't be wasting money on dry cleaning this year.'

'But won't it be an awful lot of work for you? Surely you should be resting?' Jack said, without turning round, giving all of his attention to unhitching the second curtain at a steady pace.

'I feel absolutely fine,' I said, vigorously shaking another cushion free of its cover and adding it to the pile. 'In fact, better than I've felt in absolutely ages, and I've got my mother here to lend a hand. I'd just as well make full use of her while I can.'

As if on cue, she wandered into the room and looking round in astonishment, she demanded, 'What on earth is going on? Are you mad, Jack, expecting Fay to be washing curtains and cushion covers with the baby due to arrive practically at any minute?'

I watched him shrug, though he didn't turn round as he told my mother in a resigned tone, 'This isn't my idea, Iris, I can assure you of that. Perhaps you can try and talk some sense into Fay because I certainly can't and, yes, I have already tried.'

She turned to me, tightened the belt of her towelling robe, straightened her back and gave me a look that might have had me quaking in my shoes – if I was still ten years old. Being quite a bit older and no longer a child, I simply returned her look with one of my own.

'I feel fine, better than I have for quite a while, as I've just been telling Jack and I don't need to remind you that I won't have time to do this sort of thing once the baby is here.' I straightened my own shoulders and added, 'You can help me or not, but I'm determined to get as much as I can done today. Tomorrow I might not feel like it.'

Jack turned on the step-ladder and climbed down carrying the second curtain.

'See,' he told my mother, clearly feeling vindicated, 'she's bound and determined to spring clean the whole house in a day. I would like to stay and help more, but I do have a job to go to, so I'm putting my trust in you, Iris, to keep a strict eye on Fay and make sure she doesn't do too much – or climb any ladders – and I wish you the best of luck with it.'

'Right.' My mother pushed the sleeves of her towelling robe up to her elbows. 'I can see how it is and, if you've made up your mind to scour the house from top to bottom, I will be keeping up with you and also keeping a strict eye on you. The first sign of you flagging, mind, and you'll be on that couch with your feet up and no arguments. I don't know what the midwife would have to say about this, though, I'm sure.'

I bent to pick up the pile of cushion covers and then only just stopped myself from putting my hand to my back as I straightened. It was an automatic gesture that I always felt helped to regain my balance now that my body was so distorted, but it might have been the very thing that would be pounced upon instantly by the watching pair.

I followed Jack to the kitchen and through to the utility room, calling over my shoulder to my mother, 'You might want to go and get appropriately dressed, if you're going to give me a hand.'

'I presume I'm allowed to eat some breakfast first,' she said sniffily and quite loud enough for me to hear, 'and I doubt Jack has eaten either, since you've obviously had him working since the crack of dawn.'

I came back into the kitchen, made a laughing apology, and offered, 'Scrambled egg on toast coming up for the pair of you. I've just realized I haven't eaten anything either. You just have time for a quick shower and it will be on the table.'

Jack would only take time for a couple of slices of thickly buttered toast before he left, with the strict admonishment not to overdo it and to keep the doors and windows locked.

I had no intention of overdoing anything. I wasn't that stupid, but I just shook my head at the thought of spring cleaning on such a warm day with all the doors and windows tightly closed. Jack's car had scarcely pulled out of the driveway before I was gaily flinging open windows, and feeling completely safe in the knowledge that Iona putting one foot inside the property with my mother at large would be more than her life was worth.

By the time my mother made an appearance – dressed for action in an ancient tracksuit of mine, but with her hair done and make-up on – the second lot of washing was in, the cushion covers were already blowing on the line and Betty had come round to offer her help.

'I don't know what on earth she thinks she's doing,' my mother confided in a theatrical whisper that could probably have been heard halfway down the street. 'She should be thinking of preparing for the baby's birth, not turning the house inside out.'

'I heard that, Mother,' I said, banging a plate of scrambled egg on toast onto the table in front of her. 'It's a lovely day and I feel great – you don't have to help if you don't want to.'

'That's not what I meant and you know it,' my mother came back. 'Why don't you let Betty and I get on with it? You can take it easy and just tell us what you want us to do.'

'That won't do at all,' Betty said, picking up her knife and fork and tucking enthusiastically in to what would, I was certain, be her second breakfast of the day, but enjoying it all the more because she was eating it in company. 'Fay's doing what comes naturally – we used to call "nesting" in my day.'

'Nesting?' I said, spreading honey thickly on my toast.

'Nesting?' repeated my mother. 'What's that when it's at home?'

'It's what most mums do as the birth approaches. They're subconsciously getting ready for the new baby – just as birds will nest, and most animals will look for a suitable place to give birth. Humans aren't that much different. You can't argue with a mother's instincts, Iris.'

This seemed to satisfy my mother, though she couldn't resist warning me, 'Well, all right, then, but you leave the heavy work to Betty and me, and lift nothing that weighs more than a duster.'

After a final cup of tea we set to with a will, washing what could be washed, polishing everything from furniture to floors, while the washing on the line dried in no time and Betty took charge of the ironing board.

The sun shone steadily through sparkling windows, and the breeze sent freshly laundered and re-hung curtains billowing into the pristine rooms. The fresh air, I noted, cleared the rooms of the slight mustiness of a long winter with far more efficiency than any air freshener.

Julie appeared around midday with a sleeping Oliver in his pram. She offered to make sandwiches for lunch when she saw what was going on. Briskly buttering bread, she looked over her shoulder to where I was polishing knives and forks that didn't need the attention, and laughed.

'Oh, Fay, I remember it well. I cleaned the house from top to bottom when Oliver was due and went into labour the very next day.'

'Well, I've never felt better,' I assured her, 'and I don't have so much as a twinge. It's another week until my due date.'

The back ache started when we were all sitting round the table eating our lunch. I carefully kept quiet about it, realizing I must have over-done it a bit – and that my mother would take a great deal of pleasure in frequently telling me so to the point of boring us all to tears.

'I was going to walk the dogs, if you can spare me,' Betty said, looking at me, and when I nodded, she turned to Julie with the offer to take the recently fed Oliver in his pram with her.

'Oh, are you sure, Betty?' she beamed. 'That would be great. He hasn't been asleep long and the motion of the pram together with being out in the fresh air will mean he'll sleep

a bit longer than usual. If you're sure you can manage the
dogs and the pram, it means I can help Iris and Fay to finish
everything off here. I would take the key, if I was you, and
then you can let yourself in when you come back – in case
we're working upstairs.'

I was just feeling thankful that pretty much everything was
done by this point, because the pain in my back was getting
harder to ignore and I wanted nothing so much as to lie down
with a pillow pressed to my spine.

We were in the dining room and I was doing very little
except to stand and watch my mother re-hang the curtains
there with Julie's assistance. I have no idea why it was decided
that she'd be the best one up the step-ladder – and by then I
was quite past caring. All I wanted was for the job to be done
so that we could call it a day.

I had just gritted my teeth against the quite fierce ache in
my back and made up my mind that I would really have to
say something when my mother took a step down, missed her
footing and fell at Julie's feet.

I momentarily forgot my own discomfort as I rushed to
her side. She assured us both that she was absolutely fine, but
when Julie and I helped her up off the floor and she tried to
stand, she found that her ankle was way too painful for her to
put any weight on it.

'Should we call an ambulance?' I wondered out loud.

'Oh, no, dear,' she protested, 'I'm quite sure it's not broken.'

'Probably a sprain,' was Julie's verdict, 'but you should get
it looked at anyway, Iris. It will be a whole lot quicker if I run
you down to the surgery and let the doctor take a look at it –
just to be on the safe side.'

'Oh, but that would mean leaving Fay on her own.'

'I'll make sure I lock everything up as soon as you've

gone, Mum, and I'll be fine. Betty will surely be back soon and the quicker you go, the sooner you'll be back. Really,' I said it almost desperately, 'I'll be absolutely fine. If you're that worried, I'll phone Jack.'

Her face cleared when I said that, and she urged me to do just that. She was still torn, I could tell, but somehow we got her out of the house and into the car that Julie had brought round.

'Once I've shut everything up I'll just go and sit quietly,' I convinced them, adding, 'I promise.'

The minute they were gone, I hurried round slamming windows and doors shut and then, with a deep groan, I lowered myself onto the couch, banking cushions behind me and pulling a throw over me. The pain was quite vicious and I couldn't think for the life of me what I might have done in the space of just a few hours to damage my back and cause so much discomfort. A pulled muscle, perhaps, but whatever it was, in spite of the gnawing ache, I was so tired from my efforts of the morning that I did actually manage to doze off.

I wasn't sure how long I had slept, or what it was that had woken me, but I was certain I couldn't have been asleep that long because the sun was still streaming into the room. In fact it was so bright in my eyes that I had to close them against it.

I felt so much better for the sleep but, as soon as I tried to move, the pain surged back and cut through me like a knife. It seemed to consume my whole body, taking my breath away. I had never known discomfort quite like it and it was all I could do not to groan out loud.

Eventually, it seemed to ease and I managed to sit up, give myself a mental shake, gather my wits and take in my surroundings. The first thing I noticed was that the curtain was blowing into the room, just as it had been earlier in the day, and even as I felt a certainty that I had closed it before taking to the couch, I became aware of something else. Someone was sitting in the room with me – and I suddenly knew without turning my head exactly who that someone was going to be.

Chapter Twenty

Iona looked ... I paused and thought about how she looked for a moment – despite my shock at finding her sitting there – but that she was *different* somehow was all that I could come up with. Band-box fresh in a linen dress of palest grey that brought out the steely tone of her eyes, and over the dress she wore a little bolero style black jacket. The killer-heeled shoes on her narrow feet were also black and so was her large handbag.

She must have been outside, watching and waiting, and then had snatched her chance the moment it occurred. That she clearly was never affected by nerves, when she was planning her actions, was apparent in the make-up that had clearly been expertly applied with a steady hand, and the smoothness of long black hair that hung as straight and shiny as satin ribbon onto her slim shoulders.

Though it was very much against my will, I couldn't help but admire such perfection, and found that I could only question again why Jack would have chosen me over her – with or without the additional enticement of a baby added to my side of the equation.

Iona sat patiently, waiting for me to collect myself, or so

I imagined. I tried to concentrate and to ignore the pain that held me viciously in its grip once again. I had never known a backache like it and wondered at the likelihood of a slipped disc. I didn't speculate about why she had come – I just wished that she would leave, and the sooner the better.

'What do you want?' I finally managed through gritted teeth when it became clear she wasn't going to be the first one to speak.

'What do I want?' she repeated, slowly and deliberately. 'Well, I think you know the answer to that as well as I do, but ...' she paused for so long that I thought she wasn't going to continue. I shifted uncomfortably and willed her to get on and say what she had come to say and go. Then she smiled, and I blinked. 'I think we both know that on this occasion I won't be getting what I want.'

'Jack,' I said, and it wasn't a question.

Iona nodded, pouted, and threw me a look that – if I hadn't known better – I might have imagined held more than a hint of admiration. 'I don't know how you did it,' she admitted, her tone rueful, 'and it really pains me to have to admit it – but you've won, Fay.'

'Have I, though? Have I really?' I shrugged. 'What exactly have I won? A husband who found it all too easy to cheat on me – I'm not sure that's what I want or need in my life.'

'Be careful what you say,' she said her tone flat and hard, 'because if I thought it was true that you're no longer sure that you want Jack, I wouldn't be admitting defeat now. You're wrong, so wrong. Your husband didn't find it "all too easy to cheat on you" at all, and you can take that from someone who knows.

'I just wish I had accepted sooner how much Jack cares for you and saved myself a lot of grief. He's always loved you, he always will love you – though,' she looked me up and down scathingly, 'I have absolutely no idea why – but you would be a total fool to throw that away.'

'You're entitled to your opinion.' I suppressed a shudder as a fresh wave of pain swept through my body.

'You've had one blip in your perfect life, Fay,' she said harshly, 'because that's all I ever was. I'd advise you to get over it and realize how lucky you are. Despite my very best efforts, Jack has chosen you and, to be honest, I always knew in my heart that he would.

'You have it all,' she went on. 'You have Jack, your family and your friends – oh, yes, I've seen how they gather round to protect you – and soon you will have your baby, too. I've envied you. You'll never know how much I've wanted what you have – the charmed life you live and the doting husband. I wanted it so much that I tried to steal it but, sadly, it hasn't worked – and you can't say I haven't tried my damndest.'

I took a deep breath and the pain receded. 'You,' I told her, 'have no bloody idea about my life or even Jack's, or what we have gone through to get to this point. You probably think we lived the high life until we were ready to start a family and then I got pregnant right away.

'That couldn't be further from the truth, you know, because this isn't my first pregnancy – far from it – but it is the first baby I've managed to carry to full term. I could give you numbers.' I shook my head. 'They would mean nothing to you, but to us each one was a heart-breaking loss from which it was hard to recover and find the strength to try again.

'The fact I've got this far with this pregnancy is no thanks to you and your wicked persecution of me, Iona.' I thought she paled, but it was difficult to tell under the mask of make-up and I continued relentlessly. 'You could have had the demise of a dearly wanted child on your conscience – did you ever give a thought to that – or indeed to anyone other than yourself? We've been to hell and back,' I ground out, 'but I thought we had pulled through – even before I found out I was pregnant – until I found out about you.'

If I'd thought my words would pierce her hard outer shell, she proved me wrong with her next words. 'My heart bleeds,' she said it coldly, 'but affairs don't happen for no reason – even you must know that – and for a while Jack gave in to temptation,' and then she asked, suddenly and completely out of the blue, 'have you never been tempted yourself?'

I couldn't control the heat that swept my cheeks and Iona stared at me. 'Ah,' she said, 'not quite the Miss Goody-Two-Shoes you would have us believe then. Does Jack know?'

'Nothing actually happened,' I insisted, 'but, yes, Jack does know.'

I stifled a groan as a sudden sharp pain stabbed at my insides and, at the same time, I felt a surge of wetness spreading beneath me. It took a moment to realize my waters had broken and only then did it become clear that the pains I'd been putting down to backache were actually contractions as my body prepared to deliver my child into the world.

I was shocked, but immediately determined that I could not, would not, give birth to my baby under the cold grey gaze of that woman. Thankfully, so far she seemed unaware of my discomfort and the throw I still had over me concealed the amniotic fluid that continued to seep from me.

'I'd like you to leave,' I said, keeping my voice steady and my expression carefully bland, 'now.'

To my amazement and infinite relief, it appeared that Iona was going to do just that as she rose to her feet. The movement was graceful and unhurried, and I was already breathing a sigh of relief when I noticed she was opening her handbag and reaching inside – and all the time that hard grey gaze, full of loathing, never left my face.

I wanted to get to my feet, to run for the door but, in the grip of the fiercest contraction yet, I could do neither. All I could do was sit and tighten my grip on the cushions on either side of me. I swallowed a deep groan and fought against the urge to bear down as my baby struggled to be born, and I was forced to wait and see what it was that Iona had concealed in her bag. It was obvious to me now that she had come here to kill me because of course, being Iona, if she couldn't have Jack, she was going to make damn sure that I couldn't, either.

'I came here today to tell you,' she began as she pulled out ... her *passport,* and added bluntly, 'that it's over and you've won. I'm leaving the country. Thankfully, the timely offer of a job overseas that I would be a fool to turn down, has saved me the indignity of being served with the injunction I know is on the way to being processed as we speak.'

Relief swept through me, immediately followed by another huge wave of the all-consuming pain of childbirth. I didn't think I was going to be able to remain silent for very much longer. Already incapable of speech, I could only squeeze my eyes tightly shut, biting down hard on my lip until I felt the flesh tear and then a trickle of blood on my chin.

When I opened my eyes again it was to find I was alone – alone and about to give birth. A first time mother who hadn't attended any of the preparation classes or read very much at all of the literature I'd been swamped with, and all because I was, quite simply, too scared to accept that I really was pregnant in case I would never get this far.

Vaguely aware of a door opening and closing, I decided that if it was Iona returning I had no choice but to put our many differences aside and call on her for assistance.

'I don't know what's the matter with that dog,' I heard Betty saying from what seemed like a very long way off, 'but I'd barely reached the park before Gemma wanted to come home. I'm really quite cross with her and I've made her go indoors with the others, because that wee baby has had very little fresh air and the other dogs have missed out on a proper wal ...'

I felt rather than heard her come into the room. She must have been momentarily shocked into silence but, obviously taking in the situation at a glance she was beside me in an instant and taking charge.

'Now don't you worry, my love, I'm here with you and I know exactly what to do.'

'That's more than I do then,' I muttered, as she helped me to roll from the couch to the floor, where she tore off and discarded my lower garments with speedy efficiency and made me as comfortable as she could.

'I should get some help,' she told me, 'phone for an ambulance – though I doubt it will get here in time now.'

I gripped her hand and groaned. 'No, don't leave me, Betty. Don't leave me alone.'

There was just Betty and me; pain that made me writhe and sweat and a body that felt as if it was being torn in two.

The front door slammed and Julie's bright voice called, 'We're home. It was a sprai...'

I felt Betty's enormous sigh of relief before she interrupted the cheerful flow of words, to shout urgently, 'In here, in here – quick as you can,' and then, 'towels, lots of them – as many as you can find – some to put underneath Fay and some for the baby. Boil water, plenty of it and get me scissors and some string. Oh, and someone ring Jack – and tell him to get here *now* – and an ambulance.'

There was a stunned silence, and then another groan from me brought the sound of scurrying footsteps as there was an audible rush to do Betty's bidding. Piles of white towels arrived as if by magic and, in spite of my protests, I was rolled back and forth by willing hands until layers of towels were beneath me.

'We shall be fine now,' Betty assured me, sounding far less ruffled now that she had things under control.

'But where's Jack?' I fretted. 'He should be here. He should be he-e-e-re.' The last word turned into a wail, and I found myself heaving and grunting in an effort to get the child out into the world.

'That's it, my love,' Betty crooned, 'you're doing really well and baby is nearly here. Just do as your body tells you and you won't go far wrong. You want to push, you go right ahead.'

'What on earth is going on here? Why is there an ambulance pulling up outside?'

The sound of Jack's voice had me struggling to sit up, despite Betty's best efforts to restrain me.

'In here, Jack, in here,' I managed, before I had to give all of my breath and my energy to pushing with all my might.

'Oh my God.' He was on his knees beside me in a moment. 'What's happening – is it the baby?'

'If it isn't ...' I found a wry smile from somewhere. '... I think I'm in trouble.' And then I saved my breath, gritted my teeth and pushed until I was sure I must be purple in the face.

'There, that's the head.' Betty's voice was full of excitement as she encouraged. 'Now just pant and go with the next contraction and here comes baby....'

I felt another rush of amniotic fluid and the slither of the child leaving my body and I waited expectantly for the cry that told me everything I had been through was worth it. There was nothing, nothing at all but an eerie silence.

In that moment I knew it had all been in vain. I had been right all along to keep my hopes and expectations low. Given my long and sad history of failed pregnancies, I should have known that this time would be no different.

I had been straining to see the child I had delivered but now I lay back on the hastily arranged towels and weak tears trickled from my eyes. Looking at the shocked and saddened faces of Betty and Jack, I finally acknowledged something that I should have accepted a very long time ago – that I was never destined to be a mother.

'No.'

I thought the anguished cry had come from my lips, but it was Jack who, with a broken-hearted sob, rose to his feet, snatched up the silent body of our still-born child and wrapping it in a towel, ran with it out of the door.

Betty and I didn't move. We just stared at each other, too shocked to do more than grip each other's hands and stay there in silence – waiting for what, we weren't quite sure – and then, unbelievably, we heard the unmistakable wail of a new born infant.

Seconds later a paramedic came through the door, followed closely by a euphoric Jack. As the smiling medic dealt with me, Jack told me, 'We have a little girl, Fay, and she's just beautiful.'

'But she was …'

The paramedic jumped in quickly to explain, 'She was just in need of a bit of oxygen to get her lungs working, and now she's waiting in the ambulance for you to join her for a trip to the hospital, just so that the pair of you can be given the once over.'

It seemed only moments – but it had, in fact, been many years and many heartaches – before I finally held our baby daughter in my arms. Jack and I looked at each other and then into the eyes of the child who was our future – and I think that was when we both heard the click as the door to the past closed firmly behind us.